Invisible Jane

by

Anne E Thompson

Anne E Thompson

Published by The Cobweb Press
www.thecobwebpress.com
thecobwebpress@gmail.com

ISBN 978-0-9954632-3-3

For my mother - who taught me how to laugh.

Chapter One

Mr Bobb duly arrived twenty minutes after their pre arranged time on Friday evening. A series of loud rings on the doorbell announced his arrival - and woke Christopher. Jane went upstairs to placate him, while Peter led the builder into the kitchen. When Jane came downstairs, she found them both at the kitchen table.

"Hello there young Janey!" shouted Mr Bobb, "I've heard all about you and young Peter here. Sure I can help you with your project. I expect you'll be putting that kettle on shortly won't you." He gave her an open mouthed grin, obviously satisfied with his ability to take charge.

Jane smiled weakly. "Hello Mr Bobb, would you like tea or coffee?"

"Only ever tea my dear, only tea. With sugar – unless you're offering somethin' stronger of course!" he bellowed.

The thought of the overly loud, too familiar, large Mr Bobb being slightly inebriated was not a happy one. Jane moved to the kettle and began selecting mugs. Chunky holiday mugs for her and Peter and a purple one that Daphne had rescued from a charity shop for Mr Bobb. Jane was determined that her lips would never drink from that mug again. She poured steaming water over teabags and stirred them slowly before flopping them into the empty margarine tub that served as a compost bin. She added milk and carried the mugs to where the men were engrossed in conversation.

Peter looked up briefly to smile his thanks.

"Sugar Mr Bobb?"

Jane watched as Mr Bobb dumped three spoonfuls of sugar into his drink, giving them a perfunctory stir. His hands were large and calloused, with grey hair sprouting from leathery skin. Jane sat opposite the men and sipped the tea. She knew her presence was required, if not her opinions. Then Peter could tell himself that she was happy with the project, and had been part of it throughout.

Peter was explaining that they wanted an extra room, built behind the utility room and accessed from the hall. Mr Bobb was able to supply the name of a draughtsman who could also apply for planning permission. He thought he could give a fairly accurate quotation based on Peter's description. Jane watched and listened.

Everything about Mr Bobb was large. Only his cream coloured shirt was not over-sized, the discoloured buttons straining to contain the bulbous mass of the man. His hair was grey, thinning at the back, and his great hands dwarfed the mug he was holding. Jane tried not to imagine having Mr Bobb in her home for six weeks. The consolation of him being outside most of the time was undermined by the sheer volume of the man. The rather dubious appeal of an extra room was quickly diminishing, but she could sense Peter's enthusiasm growing. As they discussed depth of footings and colour-matching bricks, the anticipation was definitely one of 'when' not 'if'. Any doubts of his whim becoming a reality had been dispelled.

As if on cue, Christopher's door slammed.

"Excuse me," mumbled Jane, eager to escape, "I think Christopher must have woken up again."

"Little Tyke!" boomed Mr Bobb, "Expect he wants to be down 'ere with the men."

2

Jane smiled wanly and headed for the stairs.

#

Christopher's door was firmly closed, an indication that he was hoping not to be observed. When Jane peered into the twilight she could see a lump of duvet on the floor with pink feet extending from one end. The heap was very still.

"Christopher?" Jane whispered.

"I'm asleep," came the rather muffled answer and the feet disappeared beneath the cover. Jane crept into the room and gently lifted the quilt. Christopher and a selection of cars were hunched on the floor. His eyes were screwed shut and he appeared to be holding his breath.

Jane knelt beside him and rubbed his back.

"Come on Chris, back into bed. It's still night time and it's very late." She gently lifted the warm bundle onto the bed and smoothed the cover over him. "I'll sit with you for a few minutes."

Eyes heavy with sleep, Christopher reached for her hand and drew it to his cheek. He was very warm and tendrils of sandy hair stuck damply to his forehead. He epitomised contentment and comfort, and the mood was strangely contagious. Jane felt herself relax onto the bed as the tensions of adulthood drained silently away. She leant back against the wall, listening to the calm rhythm of her child's breathing.

The room was suddenly illuminated as Peter turned on the security lights in the garden. Christopher sighed but remained motionless and Jane guessed he was already asleep. He had not out grown the ability to move between wakefulness and deep sleep in seconds. She rested awhile, gazing around the familiar room. The curtains were thin, allowing all but the darkest corners to be seen. Her eyes wandered along the freeze of cars, their bright colours muted now to grey and indigo. She had applied the blue paint to the walls herself and could see the beetle like splodge where the

3

brush had touched the ceiling. She still planned to cover it in white emulsion despite the two year interval already passed. There was a large trunk on the floor, its lid never properly closed. A pirate hat, a coverless book and a snake of orange string dangled from the edge. On the white chest of drawers were car shaped frames holding photographs of Christopher as a baby and one of Abigail proudly clutching her new brother and beaming at the camera. The floor was littered with small metal cars, like a miniature scrap yard. A select few had been positioned to one side, lined together as though about to race.

Voices filtered into the room. Peter's was quietly muffled and Jane could imagine him walking the line of the unbuilt walls, placing unformed windows at specific heights. Mr Bobb could be more plainly heard. His voice was authoritative as he advised his junior customer, warning him of the perils of unforeseen expenses, the impossibility of predicting all the costs. His tone was pessimistic whenever discussing finances and positively exuberant when describing the quality of his workmanship. He fully believed the one small room would be standing firm in hundreds of years hence, a monument to his superior building skills and thorough expertise. He spoke darkly of those cheaper, less scrupulous characters eager to undercut prices and forfeit quality.

Jane heard their voices taper off as they strolled the perimeter of the house and back to the front door. She rose from the bed and breathed one last deep smell of Christopher before going to meet them.

She opened the front door to see Peter shake Mr Bobb's hand.

"Goodbye Mr Bobb, nice to meet you," Jane lied, cheerful because he was leaving.

"Bye then Janey. You keep that kettle handy and me and young Matthew will put that extension up in no time. You'll see!"

4

With a last sweeping wave to Peter, the builder climbed into his dirty Mercedes ("And how does he afford that?" wondered Jane) and pulled out of the driveway.

Peter bounded back inside and enfolded Jane in a bear hug.

"That went really well," he beamed, "I think Mr Bobb will do a really good job for us. He seemed very happy with all my plans."

They wandered into the house and Jane produced two rather limp salads from the fridge and added a grey sausage to each. Peter watched with faint resignation while opening a beer. They sat facing each other across the scratched pine table. Peter added a small mountain of pickle to his plate, hoping to temper the general dry despondency of the dinner. Jane took several large swallows of Peter's beer. She did not care much for the taste but felt she needed her senses dulled a little. For a while they were both silent, the mood of the food dampening Peter's enthusiasm. Jane was unsure how to mount her defences.

"Peter, we will be getting quotes from other builders won't we?" she said, "It is normal to have two or three other quotes and then choose the builder we prefer."

"Of course," reassured Peter. "Mr Bobb said to get some more quotes for comparison and then he will match the most sensible."

He leaned towards her, enthusiasm flooding back. "I'm glad this is going so well Jane. He is a bit of a character isn't he?" Peter chuckled, "I'll have to phone Tom later and thank him for recommending Mr Bobb. He's done several renovations to Tom's various properties and he speaks very highly of him. I think he's someone we can really trust."

"Yes...." countered Jane, "but he might not necessarily be easy to have around. There may be other builders who are just as skilled but less....." she paused, searching for the right phrase. "Less, well, less dominant."

Peter squeezed her hand affectionately. "Oh Jane, you do worry! Really this will be fine. I've got a good feeling about this." He pushed his plate decisively to one side and rose from his seat.

"Most of the work will be outside. You'll hardly see Mr Bobb or this chap Matthew. Now, I think I'll just call Tom." He left, keen to speak to someone who would agree with his plans.

Jane sighed as she stretched to retrieve his plate and carry it to the sink. She had lived through these decisions before. Her choices were simple. She either remained compliant and Peter carried out his plans in happy ignorance of her views; or she let her feelings be known and suffer the consequences. There would follow several tense discussions while Peter tried to convince her that her feelings were unreliable or wrong. These would become increasingly fraught until recriminations spilled into other areas of their lives. Peter would become politely frosty for several days. He would then carry out his plans with the air of a wounded and much maligned 'Leader of the Family'.

Jane sighed with the whole of her body. Having Mr Bobb in and around the house would be akin to living with a loud and odorous bear. There seemed to be no escape. She slowly tied the tea towel into knots then flung it at the toaster.

For a fleeting moment she considered making a fuss, crying, burning down the house - or even trying to persuade Peter. Instead, she left the kitchen. She told Abigail to turn off the television and go to sleep. She unpacked the ironing into the airing cupboard. She threw a lone sock into the laundry basket. There was nothing to be done but endure all the unpleasantness until it expired. With resignation, Jane completed her chores, and curled in a chair with a book.

#

True to his word, Peter duly telephoned three other local builders. They quietly visited, were polite and unassuming and left a variety of quotes. Peter looked at the figures with interest then spoke to Mr Bobb, who was outraged at the cheapness of the lower quotes, warning of shoddy workmanship and cowboys who add on extras at the last minute. Peter employed him.

There were a few weeks of stillness while plans were drawn up and submitted to the council for planning permission. It seemed to be a long drawn out process for one small room.

Finally the day Jane had been dreading arrived. Peter whistled his way around the house with an aura of contained excitement. He had offered advice in liberal quantities as to how Jane should deal with Mr Bobb. He now seemed oblivious to her sullen face and sharp replies.

Jane delivered Abigail and Christopher to their schools with even less grace than usual. She then busied herself by heaving armfuls of linen off the beds and sorting it into snowy mountains on the landing ready for washing. It was hard to settle, and she was unsure when the builder would actually arrive.

At 9:30 am the doorbell rang six times. With teeth set in the approximation of a smile, Jane went to open the door.

"Hello there young Janey! We'll be needing a key for this door so we can reach some electricity. Are you ready for us Deary? I expect you'll be putting that kettle on now won't you. You know I like tea, and Matthew here is a coffee man."

Jane looked around Mr Bobb to glimpse his employee and for the first time began to approve Peter's decision. Matthew was decidedly easier to look at than Mr Bobb. He was not especially tall but constant physical work had proved as effective as hours spent in a gym. His dark hair curled towards his eyes and he self consciously pushed it back as he smiled at Jane. She felt herself smiling back at him.

He looked, she decided, like a very clean Greek god. With arms. (Her only knowledge of Greek gods was that their statues

7

never seemed to have arms.) And he was tanned - not white marble. And probably, under the dirty tee-shirt he had a neat row of muscles. And his eyes twinkled, and - Mr Bobb was still talking.

"We'll be doing a bit of tidying up today and we'll start the hard work tomorrow. Digging. Now, where are your storm drains Janey?"

He looked at her enquiringly, fully expecting her to have heard the term before, and to be able to precisely point out their location.

"Er, I don't really know," she offered lamely. "Shall I phone Peter and ask?"

"No need for that," said Mr Bobb. "Matthew here can find them later. We'll get started. Shall we go through the kitchen?" He began to step inside.

Jane moved aside to avoid being stepped on. "You might find the side path more convenient," she offered, avoiding lumps of mud that now speckled the carpet. He did not appear to have heard.

She followed Mr Bobb into the kitchen and filled the kettle as he opened the door into the garden. She watched as Matthew walked past the window, carrying a battered radio. She reached for the purple mug for Mr Bobb then hesitated. She could hardly give Matthew a Valentine mug and Bugs Bunny did not quite suit his image. She perused her mismatched collection of mugs, acquired over the years filled with Easter eggs, or received as free gifts from catalogues. She settled on a smart green mug of unknown origin which she sometimes drank her morning tea from.

When she carried the steaming mugs outside she found the radio perched on an upturned bucket and the garden full of Radio 2. Mr Bobb was marching across the patio, shouting directions to Matthew who appeared not to be listening, as he was using a mobile phone. He looked up at Jane and smiled. It was, she reflected, the sort of smile that young girls dream about. She

8

decided not to smile back and went back into the kitchen, knocking her elbow on the doorframe as she hurried inside.

#

The day passed uneventfully. Every hour, almost to the minute, Jane would be hailed to the kitchen and informed of Mr Bobb's near death from dehydration. She watched her supplies of tea and coffee diminish and realised a supermarket trip would soon be necessary.

When it was time to go to playgroup, she left a key, as instructed, in case Mr Bobb needed anything while she was gone. She decided not to think about him being in her house without being there to supervise him. Christopher was delighted to find the men there when they got home, and spent the afternoon sitting on the bucket, next to the radio. Jane decided he was safe enough, and went to do some housework.

After being asked for the twentieth time, "What's that?" Matthew and Mr Bobb stopped answering but they seemed happy enough with the audience. He held a stick, which he beat against the bucket in time to the music. Mr Bobb seemed to approve the extra noise it created.

When Abigail returned home she peered at the builders from the kitchen door but remained aloof, refusing to ask what they were doing or to join Christopher who tried to tempt her outside. She took her homework and a supply of snacks into the lounge and sat especially close to the television.

At six o'clock, the men left. They did not announce their departure but Jane heard the Mercedes' door slam and went to the door. Mr Bobb saw her and lifted an arm in salute.

"Bye bye Janey. We'll be back tomorrow, bit earlier than today I think," he bellowed from the open window.

9

Jane waved and shut the door, noticing that Matthew drove a smart red sports car. She wondered again how much Peter was paying them.

Later, enjoying the silence, she slipped into the garden and surveyed the devastation. Max came with her, sniffing the foreign tools, exploring the rearranged space. Her much loved jasmine had been razed to the ground, the delicate branches heaped to one side. The patio, which ran the length of the house, was now bare of stones, many of which had cracked or snapped during their removal. They now formed a rubble mountain where once a rhododendron had blossomed. Jane sighed. She supposed that some damage was inevitable, and she collected two dirty mugs from the upturned bucket and went back inside to find Christopher.

His bedroom was tidy and Christopher, clean from his bath was presiding over a class of soft toys leaning precariously against the wall. He was diligently showing them all the pages of a picture book and emitting large sniffs. Jane assumed Mrs Brown at playgroup suffered from hay fever. She scooped him into her arms and bounced him heavily onto the bed.

"You're squishing me!" he giggled, wriggling to escape.

Jane breathed his soapy clean skin and sat up. She said his goodnight prayer and kissed his cheeks, absorbing his smooth skin, the perfection of his features. He smiled up at her, and she felt the almost physical bond that joined them, that immense surge of love, formed at birth and never broken.

"Night night my love," she whispered.

"What does Bugger mean?" asked Christopher.

Chapter Two

The following day at six thirty a.m. Jane and all fellow residents of Chestnut Close were awakened by the loud revving of engines. Jane groaned and sank deeper into bed. Eyes firmly closed, she heard Peter plod to the window and pull back the curtain.

"It's Mr Bobb," he announced unnecessarily, "and a young chap. They seem to be unloading a mini digger from a lorry." He began to dress, moving towards the door. "I'd better see what they're up to. You stay asleep and I'll bring you some tea."

"Stay asleep," echoed Jane, "stay asleep…"

Mr Bobb's voice was now dominating the sound waves. Someone had extinguished the engine, but there was no reduction in general volume. The redundant alarm clock filled the room with early morning radio banter. Jane reached to turn it off. Her mind was heavy with sleep. Why, she wondered, were beds so gloriously comfortable whenever it was time to get up?

She could hear Christopher chattering, asking Peter about the small red digger that had appeared in their front garden. His voice was high and urgent, enquiring as to how big Peter thought a person would have to be to be able to drive it. He was informed that he probably missed the mark by an inch or two.

"Prob'ly I can just sit in it then," Jane heard, as another door slammed. Their voices came nearer, accompanied by Peter's heavy tread on the stairs. Jane braced herself as the door opened. Her day had begun.

Despite the early start Jane was later leaving the house than usual. Christopher needed to be constantly prised from the window, as breakfast and dressing did not even begin to compete with men digging holes. Abigail pronounced herself unable to eat anything with "that noise" in the garden, or with "that man" in the kitchen asking if the kettle had boiled yet.

11

Jane eventually dumped mugs of coffee in the garden, two grumpy children in the car and shut the dog in the kitchen. He gazed through the window in disappointment as the car backed from the drive, narrowly missing the postman. Jane squeezed the steering wheel hard, breathed deeply, drove to school.

#

She arrived home somewhat calmer. She had waved politely at all the drivers who saw fit to beep at her and smiled distractedly at all the right people at both schools. As she drew level with the house she noted a large skip now filled the driveway, so she parked in the road. A light rain was falling as she hurried across the muddy path to the house.

On opening the door to the back garden, she was surprised to see a mosaic of trenches where once her lawn had been.

"Ah Janey m'dear," hailed Mr Bobb, "We've had a spot of trouble finding your storm drains. Don't know what these planners were about. Don't you worry though; we got the buggers in the end. Thirsty work mind, so I 'spect you'll be out with some drinks."

Jane retreated into the kitchen. She wondered if any of the garden would survive the onslaught and whether Peter had budgeted for landscaping. Her thoughts were disturbed by the door opening, the steaming body of Mr Bobb loomed in the doorway.

"Thought I'd come and collect those so you don't get wet. Raining harder now Janey, so we'll have to sit and wait in that shed of yours. Oh dear, look at the mud on these shoes, that's not going to help your cleaning is it? Never mind, I'll tell Matthew not to come in anymore 'til it's dry again. We can manage without using your little boy's room for a bit. Don't you worry. You won't even know we're here."

Jane passed him the mugs and caught the dog as he plodded towards the muddy outdoors.

"Er, about the lawn…" she began. "Do you think…"

"Now Janey," interrupted Mr Bobb. "Young Peter doesn't want to be paying for us to tidy up, does he? He'll put your garden right for you when we've gone. You women, you do worry," he chuckled.

He waved a mug in salute, apparently not noticing the tea that slopped onto the floor, and returned to what remained of the garden.

Jane cleared the breakfast table into the dishwasher, then wiped and mopped the kitchen floor. She considered locking the back door but decided that mere locks were no match for Mr Bobb. She rinsed a milk bottle and returned it to the front step on her way upstairs. She stopped in the hall when she noticed the answer machine flashing.

Daphne had left a rather breathless message. She was visiting a cousin on the south coast and would call in for lunch with Jane.

"No worries if you're out all day my sweet," her mother's voice said, "but if you're free we can have bit of a chat and I'll see your building works. I'll be there at twelve."

Jane glanced at her watch. It was nearly 10 a.m. so she had at least three hours, punctuality not being something that Daphne felt ensnared by. She decided to go to the bakers. Daphne would be content with stale bread, but her domesticity was inferior to even Jane's and her daughter tried to feed her vaguely nutritious food whenever she visited. Jane smiled. It would be nice to see Daphne.

#

Daphne arrived at 1.30. Jane opened the door to receive a warm hug. She squeezed her mother, kissed her brown cheek and ushered her inside. She was perplexed to notice, as she shut the door, that the step was clear of milk bottles.

Daphne dumped a small suitcase and a bulging carrier bag on the hall floor and peered into her daughters face.

13

"Too pale," she pronounced, "and tired. Are you coping darling?"

Jane smiled into the concerned eyes. "I'm fine, Daphne. Really I am. The children are well, and Christopher loves watching the builders. Peter is working long hours but that's nothing new and he seems to be enjoying it. And it's lovely to see you - come and see the mess in my garden and then we can eat."

Daphne followed her daughter to the kitchen window. She surveyed the mud, the water-filled trenches, and the row of dirty mugs balanced precariously along the fence. She waved at a damp vested man as he disappeared into the shed holding what appeared to be a milk bottle. Then she turned and caught Jane's hand.

"It all looks ghastly Jane. You poor girl. But it will be lovely when it's finished. Do you want to bring the children to the flat for a while? I'm sure we would fit and Peter would survive on his own. Will you think about it?"

Jane smiled as she turned to the fridge. "We wouldn't fit, and Abi can't miss school, and we really are fine. But thank you."

Daphne pulled two trays onto the table and scattered plates and cutlery while Jane unwrapped barely cool pasties.

"These look good," observed Daphne. "Oh, speaking of Abi, I picked up some clothes for her. They're in the hall with some sweets for her and Chris to share. I did buy you some chocolate but I ate it on the train."

They carried their lunch into the lounge, sitting opposite each other.

"Dear God," thought Jane, "thank you for Daphne and that she came. Thank you that she cares. Please don't let the clothes for Abi be too awful. Thank you for the rain and that Mr Bobb has been outside all day. Please don't let wet foundations matter. And please can my grass grow again."

Daphne was watching her, so she picked up her fork and waved it towards the window.

"Do you know the forecast?" she asked.

#

Jane drove Daphne to the station when she went to collect Christopher from his friend's house. They were slightly late and the train pulled into the station as they arrived. Jane kissed her mother and watched as she climbed aboard, then turned to leave. Feeling strangely hollow she drove away.

Christopher was extremely cross to have missed Nana and considered not speaking to Jane. However, the necessity of telling her about bouncing on a sofa (yes, they *were* allowed, it was an old one) seeing the ginger kitten, loosing a sock and eating "disgusting Sue" was too great. As Jane drove she deciphered that the kitten belonged to a neighbour, lunch had been stew and the sock really was lost.

She parked within sight of the school and watched as Abigail left her friends and walked to the car. Her face held the nonchalance of a teenager but she still walked like a child. Heavy bag over one shoulder, coat in her other hand almost scuffing against the ground; her toes turned slightly inwards, and her white socks were at different heights. Her face lifted when she saw Jane watching her and her eyes sparkled. She clambered into the car, pushing her bag under Christopher's feet, neatly avoiding being kicked.

"Are we doing anything? I've got loads of homework."

Jane smiled at her in the mirror. "No, just home. Nana came and left you some clothes but I haven't checked them yet."

"Good! Did she bring us any sweets?"

There was a pause. Jane weighed up deception against admitting to the highly coloured, artificially flavoured globs, which she suspected were at home. Honesty won.

"Yees, but, I might not want you to eat too many. It's kind of Nana but she doesn't always buy healthy sweets."

"That's why they're so nice. Why are we parking right up here? Oh! I see…"

Jane had parked several houses away from their own. Mr Bobb and Matthew had parked their own cars outside the house and the red digger was now on the road, taking a further two spaces. Jane hoped she could manage to avoid and neighbours. Maybe Peter would go and apologise for monopolising the road when he got home.

She lifted a sleepy Christopher from his car seat and followed Abigail to their house. She peered briefly into the skip. Where had that chair come from?

Mr Bobb ambled up the drive towards them.

"Ah Janey! We're off now, can't do much in this rain. See you tomorrow."

Jane waved awkwardly, shifting Christopher onto her hip, and deciding not to point out that it had stopped raining mid afternoon. She opened the front door, and frowned. There, on the step was a milk bottle. It had lost its dishwasher sparkle and was now dirty with drips of… Jane bent towards it then stiffened.

Images of Mr Bobb in the shed and her unused toilet flooded sickenly to mind. She briefly considered re washing the offending article then hurried inside and shut the door. Christopher wriggled free. She was sure the dairy must sterilise them before reusing them and she could always buy supermarket milk from now on.

In the kitchen, Christopher had already found the sweets and was chewing stickily. Lurid orange dribbled onto his chin. Abigail was also chewing whilst inspecting clothes that were now strewn across the table. There was a purple knitted skirt, a green floral nightdress and a selection of cardigans. She pulled one on and rolled up the trailing sleeves.

16

"Perfect!" she declared.

"If you are a scarecrow," muttered Jane. She had never managed to dissuade her mother from visiting charity shops and Abigail was the eager recipient of many brightly coloured and shapeless clothes. Cosily expensive garments would be shunned in preference for ill-fitting cast-offs. Jane was unsure whether it was the sheer quantity of them that made them attractive or because they were from a much loved grandparent. She found the best strategy was to say little and then lose them in the bottom of the washing basket. After a few weeks they could be removed to a box in the airing cupboard and then, when all memory had faded, firmly placed in the recycling bin.

There was a tap on the door and Jane opened it to a damp Matthew holding several mugs.

"I thought I'd save you a rather muddy trip," he said.

Jane noticed his eyes crinkled when he smiled and that his hands were cold when she inadvertently brushed them taking the mugs. She wondered if she blushed.

"It's rather a mess out there, but this is the worst bit," he reassured her, "we should have better weather coming and then we can clear up a bit. Thanks for all the coffee, it's very kind of you."

Jane smiled in acknowledgement and closed the door as he left. Abigail was watching her.

"He's nicer than Mr Bobb, isn't he?" she asked.

"Yes," replied Jane, "He is."

Chapter Three

Jane woke to the alarm the next day. Peter was sitting on the end of the bed, writing. He had stayed at the bank until late the previous evening and Jane had been asleep when he got home. She had stirred enough to smell alcohol and smoke but had decided to remain asleep.

"What are you doing?" she asked.

Peter smiled at her. "Good morning. Sorry I was late again last night. I've just been in the garden - it's exciting isn't it? One or two things I need to sort out with Mr Bobb, so I'm writing him a note."

The note was already on its third page. Jane was about to suggest that Mr Bobb did not strike her as a literary figure but then stopped. The alternative to written instructions would be for her to discuss things with the builders. She decided the list was a good idea.

Her thoughts switched to what to wear. She had no specific plans for the day but decided she wanted to look nice. She threw back the duvet and moved to the wardrobe, began to sweep her clothes across the rail. Not a dress - too fancy; not jeans - too ordinary. Except - she did have some new jeans, never worn. She pulled them out. If she wore something loose, so her muffin-top-tummy didn't show, they would be perfect. She pulled them on, twisting in front of the mirror, checking her bottom looked as good as she remembered. Then she pulled on a pink top, slightly too low at the front, so she'd have to remember not to bend over when she took out their coffee or they'd get to see her bra. She had a lacy one, she'd wear that, just in case. She stripped off, and pulled on her dressing gown while she searched for decent underwear. No one would know, but she would feel better if her pants matched for once.

Peter watched her. "Why are you looking so pleased?" he enquired as she headed for the shower.

She grinned. "No reason."

#

When Jane arrived home from the school run she glanced onto the skip. Matthew had raised the sides with planks of wood to increase the capacity. She noticed Peter's note, scrumpled, nestling amongst the earth and rubble and wondered if Mr Bobb had read it.

"And where," she wondered, "did those old tyres come from?" She pushed open the front door and bent to retrieve the post.

"Ah Janey, we was wondering when we were going to get a drink!" boomed Mr Bobb.

"Hello Mr Bobb," she replied, her voice tight, "I'll just go inside."

Jane closed the door quietly but with feeling. She switched on the kettle while sorting through the letters. There were six *great offers, not to be missed*, on items she would never buy. There were two official looking envelopes for Peter, and a bill from a catalogue for clothes long since returned. There was also one addressed to her, Mrs J Woods, in a handwriting she did not recognise. It was an invitation to a reunion at Cragsgate Hill School.

She perched on the pine table, drawing her feet onto a chair and stared at the invitation. Memories of her time there as a teenager flooded back.

Cragsgate Hill was a sprawling comprehensive, one of the few purpose-built comprehensive schools of the seventies. It had been all shiny metal and blue tinted glass. There were slippery grey floors in the corridors, and scratchy brown carpets in the classrooms that caused static shocks if you touched something

19

metal. There must have been a hidden fleet of cleaners as there had been little sign of dirt and no graffiti, but the local villains had overcome this by denting the pine lockers and bending chair legs so they all rocked when you sat on them.

The teaching had been modern. That is to say, there *was* very little teaching. The pupils were encouraged to dig deep within themselves and express whatever they found. At the end of each lesson they would be handed a stack of photocopied sheets from the banished text books and sent cheerily on their way. Homework was considered outdated and therefore unnecessary.

Her friendships there had been intense. Jane recalled sharing her innermost thoughts and feelings with a variety of girls with whom she had little in common. They would pass notes during lessons, whisper in corridors and talk long into the night when staying at each other's houses. However, Jane could not recall actually liking anyone. No memories made her smile and whilst there had been lots of giggling there had been few real laughs. Jane had been too self-absorbed as a teenager to find anything worth admiring in her friends, and envy proved fickle as they grew older and migrated into adulthood.

No, she decided, as she made tea and coffee, though it may be interesting to learn of her classmates' lives, she had no desire to actually meet any of them.

#

Christopher ate very little lunch that day. He picked up the carrots with his fingers and used his fork to mush the potato into the gravy. Jane seemed distracted and he managed to slide three large pieces of chicken down to the waiting dog before she noticed.

"Stop playing with your dinner and eat it properly," snapped Jane

"I'm full up. Can I get down?"

"Eat some grapes first," insisted Jane, wiping his hands and face with a paper towel. It scratched his cheeks and he wriggled. He managed to squeeze four grapes into his cheeks before sliding from the table.

"You look like a chipmunk," smiled Jane.

"I is...." began Christopher before a grape slipped free and shot from his mouth. Max lurched forward, sniffed then backed up in disgust. Christopher giggled and nearly choked.

"You are revolting," commented Jane as she bent to retrieve the squashed fruit. "And put on your wellies," she called after his retreating back.

Christopher pushed his feet into red plastic boots and leant on the handle to open the back door. The garden was now littered with torn up cardboard, which allowed the builders to walk without slipping in the mud. Christopher was disappointed to see the red digger had gone and he plodded over to where Matthew was heaving sticky mud from a hole.

"I comed to watch," he stated.

"Hello," smiled Matthew, "has playgroup finished today then? Why don't you sit over there," he pointed to the step by the patio window, "it's less muddy."

Jane cleared away lunch and wiped gravy off the table, chair, floor and door handle. She made herself a coffee and decided to take one for Matthew. She had noticed Mr Bobb's car speeding away earlier and the kettle had been unused for a whole two hours. She found man and boy sitting together on the step. The handle had come lose from the spade he was using, and Matthew was tightening the nut.

"Sit with us mummy," invited Christopher and she slid beside him, leaning back against the window. The jeans, though smart, were cruel, and they dug painfully into her waist. She ignored the pain, and leaned back, trying to look relaxed.

"Matthew can play a trumpet!" Christopher announced.

She looked at the builder who grinned back, obviously slightly embarrassed.

"Yes I can actually," he admitted. "My dad was a music professor at Bath and he insisted that all of us learnt at least one instrument. My three brothers play too, so it gets kinda noisy when we all get together."

Jane was surprised. Why was the son of a music professor digging holes in her garden?

As if guessing her thoughts Matthew continued, "I'm a bit of the black sheep I'm afraid. One of my brothers teaches, one works with computers and one is trying to make it as a jazz musician. I just never got on at school I suppose, too easily distracted. I left as soon as I could and have been building ever since. I ought to set up on my own really but Mr Bobb is a nice old bloke and I like working with him. Company I guess, plus he has the contacts so tends to bring the work in. It can be hard to keep the cash flowing in this game.

"I think my dad has just about forgiven me now, but we didn't really speak for years."

As he spoke, Jane could feel the glass at her back vibrating. Christopher had moved away to dangle a stick in a hole and it felt oddly intimate to be sitting against the window *feeling* Matthew's voice. She wondered if she ought to move away but found she was rather enjoying the sensation. It was a long time since she had been aware of the maleness of a man. She loved Peter, would have said their marriage was a happy one if asked, but he was very familiar, no longer exciting. For too long she had been caught up in the world of small children and housework, with no time to lift her head and look up. To notice. She was noticing now. Without even looking, she could measure the space between them, know where his shoulders ended and hers began. She sat very still, watching Christopher play and enjoying the sun on her face.

"Do you play in a band?" she asked.

"No. I used to but I didn't really like it enough to go to all the rehearsals. It's just a bit of fun really. My last girlfriend hated it." He paused. "But I think she wanted me to sell it and buy her a ring. There was never going to be any chance of that. - Are you musical at all?"

"Not even a bit," laughed Jane," I can't even sing without the children complaining!"

She looked at the network of trenches. Matthew followed her gaze.

"We've finished digging now," he said, " we can start the foundations on Monday and then it all gets better. Once we start the brickwork you'll get a feel for how it will be." There was sympathy in his voice and Jane realised that he understood how much she was hating the disruption. They sat in silence for a while.

A car screeched to a halt in the front and Jane stood up. Mr Bobb rounded the corner and the garden seemed to shrink. He was clutching a large sheet of white paper.

"Ah Janey, time for more tea!" he bellowed. "And I'll need to talk to that husband of yours, time for some more cash!" He turned to Matthew.

"Now then Matt, the wifey phoned the council for us and we've got a plan of where them drains are now." He waved the paper above his head triumphantly. "Could've saved ourselves a lot of digging we could!"

Jane returned to the kitchen, deciding not to think about the wasted time and ruined garden that might have been saved *if* the plans had been collected two days earlier. She checked her watch. There was time to shop before she collected Abigail. She opened the door and called her reluctant son inside as the telephone rang. It was Peter.

"Hello love, you okay?"

"Yes," she replied, "I'm just going to the shops before I collect Abi." She wondered why she always felt the need to justify her actions when he called from work, trying to appear as busy as he was.

"That's excellent timing then, could you do me a favour? Could you withdraw a thousand pounds and give it to Mr Bobb? He just rang me. He wants cash not a cheque, the old devil! And could you get him to sign for it?"

"Sign for it?" she echoed. "I don't exactly have written receipts and I'm not sure Mr Bobb is the sort to sign for anything…"

"Just write 'received one thousand pounds' on a piece of paper and get him to sign it when you give him the cash," explained Peter. "You'll be fine. Sorry, got to dash. I might be late again tonight. Bye."

"Bye," murmured Jane to the disconnected line and replaced the receiver. She collected her cheque book, keys and purse and put them in her bag. Christopher was now seated firmly in front of the television, thumb securely in mouth. She led him protesting to the car and drove to town.

#

Having collected money, shopping and daughter, Jane returned home. She was greeted at the door by Mr Bobb, who had obviously planned to finish early as it was Friday and was somewhat irritable at having to wait for his money.

Jane led the way to the kitchen, pausing en route to tear off a piece of writing paper. She wrote at the top 'Received in cash £1,000' and passed it to the builder.

"Peter said, if you wouldn't mind, please could you sign for the money?" She passed the thick white envelope of cash towards him.

He frowned. "Most folks just trust me," he mumbled as he reached for the pen, "Can't be working for people who don't think I'm honest."

Jane felt herself redden. "I'm sure Peter trusts you," she said. "It's just that, you know, him working at a bank and everything, he likes to feel he's doing things properly."

Mr Bobb grunted and reached into his breast pocket for a pair of wire rimmed glasses which he perched on his nose. They had the effect of softening his features, lending vulnerability and giving him the air of elderly grandpa rather than bolshy builder. Jane thought it an improvement and smiled. Mr Bobb scrawled illegibly below her writing then proceeded to count carefully the wad of notes that she had given him. Trust apparently only worked one way. He straightened.

"Well that all seems in order young Janey. You have a nice weekend with the kiddies and try to keep them out them trenches," he instructed.

Jane followed him to the door. "Thank you," she called after him, "have a nice weekend."

He raised a chubby hand above his head, stomped up the driveway and squeezed into his car. With a squeal of tyres he was gone.

#

Peter arrived home that night before Jane went to bed. He was armed with a large bunch of white roses.

"For you," he declared as he kissed her nose, "to make up for all the mud.

She snuggled close, pushing her cheek against his warm neck. "And the noise," she added, "and I think Mr Bobb peed in a milk bottle."

Peter laughed. Jane carried the roses to the kitchen sink.

"They have got straight stems," pointed out Peter, referring to poorer days when he had bought her 'budget roses'. They had looked fine in the cellophane sleeve but when removed, all the stems had been bent and twisted, springing in all directions. The following day they had been devoid of petals.

Jane trimmed the ends and filled a jug of water. She pulled off the lower leaves, pricking a finger on angry thorns. She placed the flowers in the water, wishing she had inherited her mother's ability to arrange them into even shapes.

"Thank you" she said, sucking her sore finger and smiling at the delicate petals, "they're beautiful."

She carried the vase upstairs and placed it on the bedroom window sill, so she would see them when she woke in the morning. She began to move around the room, sorting clean clothes into cupboards and pairing stray shoes.

"I've been thinking," said Peter as he sat on the bed and removed a shoe, "about Easter."

"Oh yes?" said Jane, only half listening.

"I thought it would be nice to invite my parents."

"Oh," said Jane, her face neutral.

"Maybe they could come for Easter Sunday?"

"Oh," said Jane.

Peter laughed, grabbed an arm as she passed and pulled her onto the bed, spilling folded towels that were headed towards the cupboard. He pinned her down with heavy hands on her shoulders and positioned his face so it was millimetres from hers.

"Stop saying 'OH'," he ordered, "and say 'yes dear that would be nice'."

"Yes - Dear - That - Would - Be - Nice," chanted Jane robotically.

Peter dug her hard in the ribs and she squealed and giggled, while fighting to get free. He suddenly released her and sat up.

"Well I would like them to come," he sighed, "it's ages since we saw them."

Jane sat beside him and draped an arm over his shoulder. "Okay," she agreed, "I'll be nice. I'll phone and invite them."

'And lets hope they can't come,' she thought as she went to clean her teeth.

Chapter Four

Saturday passed in a blur of children's activities - buying plimsolls, helping with homework, tidying up. It had rained during the night, and Christopher was delighted to find the trenches had become temporary home to several frogs. Abigail refused to set foot outside the back door.

Sunday morning dawned cold and bright, and Peter decided he would escort Jane to church. She was surprised but pleased. Usually she took Christopher and a fairly reluctant Abigail on her own, and she was always pleased when he joined them.

The church they attended was the local Baptist chapel and Jane had chosen it for the people, not the décor. It was not dissimilar to a draughty cowshed, complete with damp smell and dust particles that danced in the sunlight that streamed through the square windows. It had a high ceiling and was cold, whatever the weather outside. Taking a cardigan to church was more important than carrying a Bible.

They sat at the back, sliding into the light oak pew, shuffling slightly to alleviate the hardness. There were cushions, embroidered in a bygone age and never washed, which were gathered possessively by the older members when they arrived and firmly sat upon. Several people turned and smiled in greeting, and Abigail left them to sit with her friend Samantha. Mrs Whorl, in matching turquoise coat and hat, ceased her subdued playing on the organ and the minister stepped forwards to the pulpit. He announced the first song, and everyone stood.

Pastor Rob was tall and dark, with a large smile and even larger teeth. Tired eyes twinkled above a large nose as he stretched out his hands and welcomed the congregation. Jane guessed him to be aged about thirty-five, with a younger wife and two extremely naughty boys. One was crawling under the pew as they all sang, while his brother surreptitiously tore pieces from the page of a hymn book, turning it into a holy serviette. His mother stood beside him, eyes closed in concentration, trying to lose herself in the song. Jane wondered if she was succeeding.

Jane watched Mrs Whorl as she played. Her head nodded up and down, keeping strict time as she forced the ancient tune out of the organ. Jane felt the original composer had probably not envisioned such a strident rendition. Beside her, Christopher stood on the pew leaning against his father's arm. Peter held the hymn book so they could both see and was laboriously moving a finger beneath each word. Christopher watched the finger.

The hymn abruptly ended and they all sat. Pastor Rob led the people in prayers and a Bible reading. Then there was a modern praise song, which Mrs Whorl played, exuding disapproval, as quickly as possible. Pastor Rob smiled at his rebellious musician and suggested a repeat.

As they sat, Peter leaned towards Jane, pointing at the lady sitting in front of them. "Do you think she got her knitting patterns in a muddle?" he whispered.

Jane looked. The elderly lady had pinned a neat circle of crochet work to the top of her head. It strongly resembled a table mat and Jane shook with silent giggles while gesturing to Peter to listen to the sermon.

The pastor was describing God's love for the world. He held a twenty pound note above his head and asked who would like it. Jane could tell from the back of Abigail's head that she was suddenly attentive. Several people were smiling, anticipating what would be said, others were using the children's talk as an excuse to check their phones. A young girl, nudged into a response by her mother, agreed that she would like the money.

Pastor Rob scrumpled the note into a ball threw it on the floor and stepped on it. He lifted it high, showing it to be wrinkled and dirty, asking, "Does anyone want it now that it's been spoilt?"

The child was still keen to receive it and when questioned responded, "Because it's still worth something."

The pastor allowed a seconds of silence, before agreeing, "Yes, it's still worth something..." He then went on to explain that people too can be spoilt and broken by experiences but they are still of value to God.

"God doesn't just like you a bit," he reminded the congregation. "He loves you enough to die for you."

Jane looked at her family. Abigail was passing a note to her friend, Christopher was running a toy car up and down his leg, Peter seemed lost in thought. Were they even listening? Did they understand?

"I want to be worth something," she thought, "I want to be worth more than just the person who wipes up marmalade and finds lost socks." She felt strangely emotional, and began to search through her bag, looking for a distraction. People would think she was odd if she cried at a talk aimed at kids. The children were leaving now, shuffling towards the door ready for their own groups. Jane watched them, saw the resignation in their body language, knew that very few actually looked forward to being there.

Rob opened his Bible, and launched into his sermon. The words washed over Jane. She liked being in church, but not for too long. Church was something she 'did', but it was best afterwards, when the duty had been ticked off for the day and she could get on with all the other things she wanted to do. Attendance was a habit - a good habit, she reminded herself - but she often found herself distracted during the sermons, waiting for them to end.

The final two hymns were announced, the children sidled back into church and people began to shuffle as they retrieved their hymn books and searched for the correct pages. Something caught Jane's eye and she looked at the front pew. Rob's wife was holding onto one boy who was trying to escape, while the other was pulling plaintively at her cardigan. He was hopping from leg to leg and obviously needed to use the toilet.

The congregation stood to sing and the pastor, noticing the problem from the pulpit, went to rescue his wife. He deftly lifted his desperate son over the pew and carried him through the front door to the toilets. He walked very tall, he liked being the one who solved problems, was a capable multi-tasker. His wife relaxed momentarily with relief; and then froze in horror.

Pastor Rob had forgotten to turn off his radio microphone. The sounds of the washroom door, opening and closing, were clearly audible over the speaker system. So were Rob's words.

"The Lord is my light," sang the congregation.

"Is it a poo or a wee?" came from the speakers.

"Then why should I fear?" sang the people, one or two looking around with puzzled expressions.

"Sit there until you've finished," echoed from the speakers.

"By day and by night," sang a rather hesitant congregation while straining to hear the next announcement.

"Bend over and I'll give you a wipe, then you can pull the flush and wash your hands."

"His presence is near," sang three deaf old ladies.

The rest of the church shook with barely restrained laughter while Mrs Whorl played valiantly to the end of the hymn.

Jane's sides ached with laughter and she dare not look at Peter.

"Mummy, what's funny?" asked Christopher, but she could only shake her head mutely. The unsuspecting minister then returned to the pulpit for the closing prayer and the service ended.

People seemed reluctant to leave the church. Jane often felt she gained as much from the post service chat as she did from the service. People sat or stood in small groups, some talking earnestly in hushed voices, others laughing. Pastor Rob stood by the door, shaking hands as people made their exit. Someone had explained to him about the microphone and Jane heard him bellow with laughter. He loved people, and accepted them as they were, faults included; and he tended to assume he was loved in return. Jane guessed it would be his wife Esther who carried the wounds of criticism on his behalf. At present she was removing a child from a large arrangement of lilies and explaining that he could not take one home.

"Shall we go?" suggested Peter. He was always uncomfortable at informal church gatherings, anxious that someone might speak to him. He found the whole open friendly chatter difficult - he had little in common with these people, so why would he want to spend time talking to them? There were better things to spend time on, and you never knew if someone particularly odd might corner you, forcing you into an embarrassing conversation you couldn't escape from. He definitely preferred the anonymity of an Anglican service, where it was possible to arrive and leave without ever having to speak to another individual.

Jane beckoned to Abigail and followed Peter to the door. Pastor Rob was engrossed in conversation with an elderly man and they slipped out unseen.

"Well," remarked Peter, "That was certainly entertaining!"

He lifted Christopher onto his shoulders as they walked to the car.

"I wanted that twenty pounds," said Abigail. "Do you think Pastor Rob gave it to that girl? And what's for dinner?"

"Roast lamb," said Jane, "assuming the automatic oven came on. And peas. And potato."

"Yukky peas!" wailed Christopher, "I hate peas!"

"Me too," said Abigail.

"Can't say I'm too keen," added Peter as he stooped to unlock the car, swinging Christopher back down to the ground.

"Then perhaps one of you would like to cook dinner next week," muttered Jane as she climbed into the car. Any peaceful feelings generated by the service had evaporated and she felt cross and resentful. Ahead of her loomed another culinary Everest with a dry and tasteless meal at the pinnacle. She felt suddenly tired and leaned back into the seat.

Peter reached across and squeezed her leg.

"You alright, my little twenty quid girl?" he asked, then started the car and drove home.

#

Jane felt somewhat happier when the daily ordeal of providing a meal was over. The lamb had closely resembled leather and the potatoes had disintegrated when cooking, leaving only hard cores that proved resistant to mashing. Only the peas had emerged pleasantly edible and no one liked them anyway. As the supermarket manufactured fruit pie and ice cream were all that anyone ate, Jane wondered why she continued with the ritual sacrifice of raw ingredients.

The afternoon was fine and bright and Peter decided that they should all go for a walk. Christopher was delighted and quickly collected his boots and the dog lead. The dog staggered towards him, swaying in time to his wagging tail. In a few short years he had changed from an energetic Tigger to an arthritic hippo, but his enthusiasm never wavered. He surveyed Christopher with adoring eyes as the child struggled to attach the clip to the collar. Jane reached to help him and called Abigail.

"Abi, are you ready?"

"Do I *have* to come?" queried the girl, who had hoped to watch television all afternoon. "I've got loads of homework and I'll never get everything done if I have to walk."

"Well….." began Jane.

"Yes!" interjected Peter. "It's a lovely day and we're all going for a walk. Hurry up and put some wellies on."

#

They set off, and were soon squelching across an abandoned field adjacent to a building site. Max paused for long sniffing detours, whilst Christopher wound his way through every available puddle. Abigail lagged behind, reluctantly enjoying the fresh air and wistfully watching her younger brother.

"You'll fall over," she said, as Christopher slid through a particularly deep puddle.

"I've lost a boot! I've lost a boot!" called Christopher gleefully. He balanced precariously on one leg, waving a besocked foot.

Peter hoisted him free while Jane removed the other boot. She watched her son stretch his arms around his father's neck, secure in his vantage point on Peter's shoulders. He rested his cheek on top of Peter's head, then giggled as a sock came free and floated down to the mud. Jane retrieved it and carried it with the two dirty boots. She watched the tangible love between father and son as they crossed the field. Their fair hair was so similar she could not discern where one head began and the other ended. Both exuded happiness, as did Abigail who was now describing to her the plans for a school outing. She nodded and smiled, not really listening. Inside, she was restless, wanting something more than this. It was lovely, very cosy, everyone contented. But inside, something uncertain had woken, something that removed her from the scene and set her apart. It wasn't enough anymore…

Chapter Five

Monday morning began badly. Jane opened her eyes to see tea in the purple mug waiting beside her bed. Peter opened the curtains and the light bruised her aching eyes. He had written another list of instructions for Mr Bobb and was telling Jane what she needed to say. She scowled at him. It was too early to function. She forced herself from her warm cocoon and picked up a hairbrush. She noticed the roses had all bowed their heads as if in defeat and their petals hung limp as old skin. Jane sighed and her morning continued.

#

When Jane arrived at playgroup her friend Suzie was waiting.

"Hi Jane, hello Chris," she greeted them. "You okay? You look a bit tired."

"I'm fine," said Jane, "Just a bit fed-up. You know how it is. I need some *fun* in my life."

"Yep, know that feeling," said Suzie. "Ooh look, here comes someone who looks like she's had a little too much fun. It's Madam Trish!"

"Shhhh, " hissed Jane, "someone will hear you."

Both women watched as the large SUV swept round the car park, looking for somewhere to stop, narrowly missing a tired mother with a pushchair. The car was new and shiny, and Jane was fairly sure that there were no crisp crumbs mouldering under a seat, nor an all pervading smell of dog. Tricia opened the door and climbed out. She too looked new and shiny, with perfect figure and perfect clothes. Everything matched, and was very tight, as if glued on. Her high heeled black boots clicked as she walked gazelle-like to open the passenger door to release Sophia. She shook smooth black hair so it cascaded down her back (Jane was fairly sure she'd practised that at home in front of a mirror), then turned and directed a lipstick mouthed smile towards the other women.

"Good morning," she breathed as she passed them in a cloud of expensive perfume.

Jane felt grubby in comparison and tried to stand up straighter. She shook her head, hoping to imitate the cascading gesture, but a stray hair caught in her mouth and she had to pick it out with her fingers.

"How can anyone have matching lipstick and nails on a Monday morning?" said Suzie.

Jane giggled, removed the hair from her mouth, and they followed Tricia to the hall door. Tommy and Christopher had raced ahead and Sophia had joined them, dark curls bouncing as she ran. The boys were pleased to see her and the exuberant trio ran in together. Jane felt a pang of guilt. Christopher had asked many times if Sophia could come and play. She was a nice enough child, sweet natured and clever. However, the thought of her attractive yet aloof mother coming into her home was not one which Jane was keen to pursue. Tricia was never openly rude to the other mothers but her looks of distain were easy to interpret. She would greet them politely enough, but should a new mother attempt to befriend her, she would soon withdraw. Her eyes would insinuate repulsion at the over-familiarity and she would look away.

Suzie had herself been snubbed in such a manner and was now unrepentant in her ridicule of the other woman. Initially Jane had admonished her friend, suggesting the apparent snobbery was due to shyness. However, the shyness was not evident with the richer parents, and Jane decided it was more fun to listen to Suzie's caustic humour than to attempt to reform her. She wasn't sure why Tricia didn't use the private playgroup in town, if she was so much better than the rest of them.

Jane picked up Christopher's abandoned coat from where he had thrown it as he ran into the classroom. She put her head round the door to check the teacher had registered his presence. Gone were the days of long goodbye kisses, and Jane missed them. She waved at her son then followed Suzie back to the cars.

"We must get together for coffee soon."

"Yes," agreed Jane, meaning it.

#

As Jane drew up at her house she saw both builders had arrived, and realised that she was smiling. She locked the door and walked past the skip.

'Where has that old sink come from?' she wondered as she entered her house and went to make coffee.

When Jane stepped into the garden she saw Matthew was busy with a cement mixer. His arms were bare, tanned and thick with muscle. Jane noticed. For a moment she wondered what it would be like to stroke one, to run her hands over the hairs, to feel the shape of him. Then she focussed on not spilling the mugs of drink and walked towards them.

Matthew saw her and smiled a greeting. "Did you have a nice weekend?" he said.

"Yes, thanks. Did you?"

"Actually, it was quite boring," he said, smiling up at her as he eased cement into an old wheelbarrow.

"I was planning to watch the rugby with some friends but they cancelled at the last minute so I spent Saturday watching telly. Not an ideal day at all."

Mr Bobb approached waving an empty bucket.

"Ah Janey," he said, "Busy day for us today. Need our tea nice and prompt we will."

Jane nodded an acknowledgement and escaped back into the kitchen.

She was struggling to remove the vacuum cleaner from the downstairs cupboard, when the telephone rang. It was the playgroup administrator. One of the assistants had gone home feeling ill, they were making Easter cards, and she wondered if Jane could spare two hours to help them. Jane briefly considered the dirty carpets and unironed shirts, and decided she could definitely spare two hours.

She grabbed keys and coat and went to the door. Matthew was reloading his bucket but came over when he saw her in the doorway. He leaned an arm on the doorpost and asked if she was okay. He was so relaxed, so at ease with himself. So completely unaware of her as anything other than a housewife. Jane smelt aftershave and soap, and took a step backwards.

"Playgroup phoned and I said I'd go in and help. If I leave the door unlocked, can you make your own drinks this morning?"

Matthew grinned. "You shouldn't take too much notice of Mr Bobb," he said, "he just likes to feel in charge. Have you got some old newspapers you could put on the floor so I don't leave footprints? Then I won't have to keep taking off my boots."

Jane assured him she had and smiled her thanks. She decided not to watch him as he returned to work.

#

Jane leaned hard on the playgroup door but it refused to open. She peered through the small square of glass and waved at Mrs Brown. The teacher strode over and unlocked the door.

"We have to keep this bolted," she explained, "Or we're in danger of losing our two runners."

Jane was greeted by the smell of small bodies, feet and powder paint. Mrs Brown ushered her inside and secured the door behind her. Small and slightly plump, she wore a flowery apron over a fawn cardigan and maroon corduroys.

"Thanks for bailing us out," she said as she led Jane over to the activity table.

"Poor Julia tried to struggle on, but I think these leering chicks were just too much for her weak stomach. Now, do you need an apron? No? Okay, we'll put you just here. If you could sit and help the children stick the body parts on in the right order. Then check if their names are on the back and send them to wash their hands in that bowl of soapy water. Shout if you need anything.

"Tamzin! Stop putting glue in James' hair!

"Come along Freddie, let's sort out this puzzle."

The teacher moved across the room, deflecting several small children as they brought her their requests and settled herself on a stained blue carpet in the corner. She sat where she could watch the whole room, while her hands deftly removed a puzzle from its box and her voice soothed the fidgeting Freddie.

Jane perched on a tiny plastic chair and slid her legs under the table. Christopher sidled up to her, delivered a rather sticky kiss and then ambled back to a large toy ambulance. The table was strewn with brightly coloured paper. A few fully assembled chicks gazed drunkenly from their cards. 'HAPPY EASTER' had been stencilled onto each one, and the children were busy dolloping glue onto the pre-folded cardboard.

"I know who you are," announced a small girl. "You are Chrithtopher'th mummy."

"Yes, that's right," said Jane, "Now, shall we put the eyes above the beak? I think it would look better."

"My name ith Tharah," continued the child "and I have got a cat. Have you got a cat?"

"Yes, I have actually"

"Well, I've got a dog," said another child, keen to join in. "Have you got a dog?"

"Yes," said Jane, "I have a dog too."

39

"Well," announced a small boy, determined not to be outdone, "I've got a verruca. Have you got a verruca?"

Jane giggled. "No," she admitted, "I haven't".

The boy smiled in triumph and glued a beak onto his chick. The glue oozed out the sides, wet and grey. He wiped it away with his finger then smeared it onto his apron.

"We made these last year too," he confided as he moved away to wash his hands.

Sophia bounded up to the table. "Hello," she said, "can I make one of them?"

"Yes of course," said Jane and pencilled her name on the back of a green card. She gathered a head, body, eyes and beak and passed them to Sophia.

"You need to put on an apron," she directed, "and then stick these onto your card. Then use the black felt-tip to draw the legs."

Sophia struggled into a red plastic apron and Jane fastened the velcro at the back, careful to avoid her soft dark curls.

"Thank you," said the child, as she collected the paper and moved to a clean piece of newspaper. She lifted the glue brush, leaving a trail of paste from the pot to her card.

"Can I come and play with Christopher today?" she asked.

"Er, maybe not today," replied Jane, "maybe I could talk to your mummy and we could arrange it for another time.

"Tomorrow?" said Sophia.

"We'll see," said Jane. She watched as a small boy put the felt-tipped pen into his mouth.

"Don't chew the pen," she said, reaching to pull it from his mouth. Black ink dribbled down his chin. He grinned at Jane, showing black edged teeth and a purple tongue.

"Oh dear," she murmured as she tested the diluted pen on the newspaper. "Have you got a tissue and I'll wipe your mouth?"

"They're on Mrs Brown's table," said Sophia. "And Michael is always doing that, aren't you Michael?"

He glared at her and went to fetch a tissue. As he went Jane noticed a suspicious damp patch on his trousers. She decided not to mention it.

Another child crept up to the table and reached for a card.

"Hello, what's your name?" asked Jane. The boy lowered his head and continued selecting pieces of paper.

"I'll write your name on the back for you," she explained, "what are you called?" The boy pursed his lips but remained silent.

"He's called George," said Sophia, "but he cant talk."

George moved to the seat next to Sophia and began sticking his chick together. She helped him glue the eyes in place, leaving sticky fingerprints on the chick's cheeks. Then she reached for the pen and boldly drew four legs on her own card. She surveyed her handiwork and smiled.

"I've finished," she told Jane, before skipping across the room to wash her hands.

Her place at the table was taken by a small boy with fair hair and a runny nose. Every so often his tongue would appear and lick his top lip. Jane offered him a tissue but he looked alarmed, so she left him to glue and sniff in peace. The verruca boy reappeared at her side.

"How old are you?" he asked.

"Well," stalled Jane, "That's not a question that you should really ask a grown-up."

The boy considered this response. In his experience, an unwillingness to answer a question was due to an inability to do so. He decided to be helpful.

"Are you more or less than a thousand?"

"Definitely less," giggled Jane. Satisfied, the boy galloped away to the sand tray.

As she helped the children with their cards, Jane looked around the room. Most of the children were occupied with toys at a table, or on the carpet. A few boys were building a tower with bricks and shouting every time someone knocked it over. There was a wooden playhouse in one corner, where the children could dress-up and reenact scenes from home. A boy in high heels and a fireman's hat was lowering a baby into a cot while a girl poured imaginary tea from a plastic pot. Mrs Brown had moved from the carpet and was now at the drawing table. She was placing dots on a child's picture so he could join them to write his name.

The noise in the room was not loud but it was constant. The other assistant ferried children to and from the toilets and swept sand from the floor so no-one slipped. Jane saw that every time her back was turned, a child with long ginger hair purposefully tipped a cup of sand onto the floor and scuffed it with her foot. She was not sure if the assistant was choosing to ignore this or had not noticed.

Mrs Brown moved to the centre of the room and clapped her hands.

"Children, please stop!" she commanded shrilly.

Most of the children instantly froze and looked at their teacher expectantly. The boys with the bricks ignored her and had to be hissed at by the assistant. When the room was silent, Mrs Brown continued.

"It's time to tidy up and have our snack. Then it will be story-time. Now, I will be looking to see who is the best child at tidying up today," she announced, staring round at her class. All the children straightened, keen to be noticed as the best. "Right, off you go...

"And Douglas, find your clothes," she added to a boy who had shed shoes, socks and shirt and was hiding under a table.

The room became a frenzy of activity. Jane moved the completed cards to the window ledge then swept the rubbish into a tall black bin. The assistant removed the glue pots to wash them, returning with a cloth to wipe the tables. Children threw toys into large plastic containers and helped push them into a corner cupboard. Jane was impressed by the total co-operation and was amazed to see Christopher's participation. She wondered why he was so incapable of tidying at home.

When all toys were away, the children sat around a table and were handed a drink and a piece of fruit.

"We used to have biscuits," said Mrs Brown, leaning towards Jane, "But too many parents made a fuss. Now we have fruit, but lots of them don't like it."

Peace descended. Jane watched as the children munched grapes and apple segments. Then her thoughts wandered to home and she wondered what Matthew was doing. She imagined him in her kitchen, making coffee, touching the kettle, the cupboards. Suddenly George spilled his drink, and she hurried in search of a cloth.

When all the children had finished, Mrs Brown moved to a chair on the carpet. The class sat at her feet and waited for a story. Jane and the assistant, who introduced herself as Shirley, cleared away the table and chairs and washed the cups. They were stacked in a cupboard under the sink that smelt strongly of mice. Jane wondered briefly if she ought to mention the possibility of rodents but Shirley was already heading back towards the carpet.

"We sit with the children now," she whispered, "and sort of encourage them all to listen to the story."

Jane joined her on the carpet. Christopher quickly plonked himself on her knee and Sophia shuffled nearer and leaned against her. She gazed up and smiled at Jane, then turned back to listen to Mrs Brown. Her weight was warm and comfortable and she smelled of cinnamon. As she listened, she reached up and pulled at one of her curls, stretching it between finger and thumb. Her eyes grew dreamy.

Michael crawled over to Shirley and clambered onto her lap. She grimaced as the warm damp seeped through her jeans and she moved him, plonking him onto the carpet beside her.

Jane listened to the tale of lost toys being rescued. She felt that, if she were a lost toy, the last thing she would want was to be given to a child, to be broken or abandoned under a bed. Her thoughts began to turn again to Matthew.

"I feel like a teenager developing a crush," she thought as she shifted her position on the carpet to allow some blood back into her foot. "How stupid….But it's only thoughts, it doesn't matter." She forced her attention back to the teacher.

Mrs Brown told the children that they could take their Easter cards home tomorrow, when they were dry.

"Mine's for Daddy," whispered Christopher.

Then the class was told to line up at the door, ready to meet their parents. It felt strange for Jane to be on the other side of the door, not to be rushing across the car park to await the opening of the door. Mrs Brown stood in the doorway, releasing the children to their carers. She called their names in turn as she spotted their waiting adult, until only Christopher remained.

"Thank you so much," she said, turning to Jane, "You were a huge help."

"You can call me any time," said Jane, "I enjoyed it. Will you need help tomorrow?"

"No, but thank you. Julia only does one slot a week, so we should be okay for tomorrow."

Jane nodded. "Bye then," she said, turning to help Christopher into his coat.

"Lets go home for lunch."

#

When they arrived home, Christopher ran straight to the back garden. He surveyed the concrete filled trenches in alarm.

"Where are all the frogs?" he asked, his voice full of concern.

"Oh, those frogs all hopped back to their pond when we arrived," said Matthew, "I don't think they liked the noise of the cement mixer."

"Tell your mum I'm nearly dead with thirst," bellowed Mr Bobb from the shed doorway. "Young Matthew makes awful tea!"

Christopher scampered inside to deliver the message. He found his mother at the kitchen table, frowning over a list.

"What do we need for Easter lunch Chris?" she sighed, "Granny and Grandad are coming so I need to be organised."

"Ice-cream..." ventured the boy hopefully, "and bananas and sausages. And a great big EASTER EGG!" he shouted. "...But none for Abi."

"Don't be mean," said Jane, standing to prepare his lunch. "I don't think I can give Granny sausages. I think I'll have to cook turkey and vegetables."

The kettle boiled and she began to make drinks for the builders. "Maybe I could buy a tub of nice gravy and frozen roast potatoes. We could have fruit pies for pudding....." Seeing her son's horrified face she added, "and ice-cream."

She left Christopher chewing a cheese sandwich and carried the drinks outside.

"You look lost in thought," commented Matthew as he took his mug.

"I'm trying to decide what to cook for Easter lunch," said Jane. "We have Peter's parents coming."

"Is that good?" said the builder, raising an eye-brow and leaning back against the fence.

"Not exactly," admitted Jane with a grin.

45

"Maybe you should ask Peter to cook," he suggested.

She laughed. "And that is a terrible idea."

"Ah Janey!" shouted Mr Bobb as he emerged from the shed. "We're parched out here."

Jane passed him his tea and returned to Christopher.

#

Peter came home earlier that evening, bringing with him a box of chocolates and some unwelcome news. They sat in the kitchen, which was warm and steamy. Peter sat one side of the table, picking at his dinner, Jane and Abigail sat the other, eating chocolates.

"They've asked me to go to New York for two weeks," announced Peter.

Jane picked out a toffee and nibbled the chocolate off the top. "When?" she said.

"On Wednesday. I'll be back for Easter."

There was silence.

Jane was annoyed, partly because she felt that he should have waited until they were alone before telling her. She put the half eaten chocolate on the table. It felt like a bribe now, so that she wouldn't make a fuss. She'd let Abi eat them.

"What did you say?" she said, knowing the answer.

He paused. "I said yes." He leaned towards her for emphasis and looked her fully in the face. "I need to go Jane. It will be good for my career and I'm lucky that they asked me. You'll be okay. I haven't been away for ages and the builders will be around, so you wont be lonely. It's brilliant timing really, when you think about it."

"But..." Jane began, then she too paused. How could she tell Peter that she was attracted to one of the builders and needed her husband to return home each night to bring some sanity back into her life? She picked up the toffee again.

46

"I find Mr Bobb difficult. And what if they do something wrong?" She swallowed, but too quickly, and felt the lump of the sweet as it passed down her throat.

Peter put his cutlery on his plate and drew back his chair.

"Look, the phones to New York work pretty well you know. I'll have my mobile on the entire time. Anyway, I trust Mr Bobb, you'll be fine. I don't know why you're making such an issue out of this. Some wives might even be pleased for their husbands and congratulate them...." He moved to the sink with his plate and filled a glass of water.

"Will you buy us presents?" asked Abigail, watching them both.

"Of course," smiled Peter, and the discussion ended.

Chapter Six

Jane barely saw Peter before he left. He worked long hours Tuesday, preparing the office for his absence, and a taxi arrived Wednesday morning before Jane had woken. She felt Peter's kiss on her forehead and wound sleepy arms around his neck.

"Take care," she murmured.

"You too. I'll phone when I get there. Love you."

Then he was gone.

When Jane got up, the house felt cold. Wherever she went there was evidence of Peter's absence. No razor on the shelf, only one toothbrush in the china pot on the windowsill. His dirty trainers, a constant source of irritation, were missing from the hall floor. As she prepared Christopher's breakfast she saw Peter's bowl resting in the sink. It was almost, she thought, as if he had died.

Abigail was having a day off school. Her teachers were having a 'training day', whatever that meant. It used to be called an 'Inset Day' and Abigail had insisted on calling it an 'Insect Day' to annoy Peter. Jane felt the teachers had more than enough days during the school holidays for training and resented the change in routine.

However, today they were to buy shoes. Suzie had agreed to collect Christopher from playgroup and Jane planned to take her daughter into the city. They could catch one of several trains and she found herself choosing one that would allow time to see the builders before she left.

Abigail emerged from her room dressed entirely in dark purple. She wore purple woolly tights beneath a purple skirt she had outgrown a year previously and which was now daringly short. A purple shirt from Daphne had been pulled in at the waist with a belt (also purple) and the sleeves rolled back to expose the purple cuffs of an old jumper. A purple scarf was wound around her head and finger nails and lips were painted to match.

"I gave birth to a witch!" thought Jane.

She was tempted to tell her daughter to change, to explain that she looked ridiculous and that a ten year old child should dress like a child, not a delinquent teenager. Many apt phrases came to mind. Instead however, as ever, she chose to avoid confrontation. It was easier to say nothing.

"Are you ready to go? Good. We'll catch the 10 o'clock train. Don't forget to clean your teeth and it's cold today, so wear your long school coat."

Abigail remained silent and moved towards the bathroom. Her eyes shone with the knowledge of a small victory.

#

As mother and daughter walked up the driveway, Matthew's car drove down the road. He flashed his lights in greeting and parked behind the skip, which was now brim full. Jane frowned at the refrigerator perched on top of the rubble.

Matthew locked his car and smiled at Jane.

"Hello, are you out again today?"

"Just to buy shoes," explained Jane. "I left the back door unlocked. You can help yourself to drinks, but please try to keep the dog in. We should be home by lunch time."

Abigail was tugging at her hand and Jane allowed herself to be pulled along the path. "Bye," she called. They began to walk towards the station.

"Matthew likes you," announced Abigail.

"I expect he likes everyone," said Jane.

"Yes, but he smiles at you all the time," said Abigail.

"I expect he's just happy to be earning so much money," countered Jane. But she felt pleased. It would be fun if he liked her.

#

They arrived at the station with barely time to buy a ticket before the train arrived. They climbed aboard an extremely full carriage.

49

They stood at one end, Jane holding on to both the luggage rack and Abigail, who refused to hold on to anything. The carriage was filled with retired people, most of whom seemed to know each other and were chatting whilst darting looks of suspicion towards Jane and her purple daughter. As the train jolted to a stop at the next station, Jane swayed onto an austere man reading *The Telegraph*.

"I am sorry," said Jane, struggling to her feet. The man merely tutted and shook his paper in annoyance.

"Honestly!" raged Jane as they disembarked and hurried from the station, "What did he have that we didn't?"

"A seat," muttered Abigail.

Jane laughed and caught her daughter's arm. They headed down the crowded streets, avoiding people in suits carrying cardboard cups of expensive coffee. They passed brightly lit chemists, and dim newsagents that smelt of curry and dust. A gaudy sign filled a window promising half-hour photography processing, and that they could unlock any phone; next door was a shop spilling plastic buckets of umbrellas onto the pavement. Warm sugar and onions wafted from a fast food cafe. A tramp was huddled into a sleeping bag, gazing at the world through glazed eyes, and a lady in stilettos was trying to remove her heel from a grate.

As they neared the main shopping precinct the atmosphere slowed. Large shop windows had been designed with care, each offering a storybook of colour and style. Cashpoint machines perched helpfully on street corners and a lone saxophonist filled the air with jazz. Fresh coffee and handmade chocolates fought with cosmetics to perfume the walkways and the shoppers became less purposeful as their senses were distracted.

"I'm starving," declared Abigail as they neared a cafe.

"Let's look in one she shop, then have a coffee stop," said her mother.

They paused in the entrance to a fashion shoe shop. Jane hovered near a stand of black leather shoes with low heels and laces.

"Ace!" said Abigail, advancing towards some platformed purple sandals. "We just have to buy these, it's a sign. Can you find my size?"

"No," said Jane, not looking up. "Do you like these?"

"They are completely disgusting. Anyway I want coloured shoes, not black."

"But you need black shoes for school," said Jane, "that's why we've come."

Abigail pouted.

"But these are so nice," she wheedled, "or those pink ones. Can I just try them on?"

"You can try them on, but I am not buying them." Jane felt a headache was likely. She entered the shop in search of black shoes that Abigail might like, while her daughter tottered behind her in two left shoes, one purple and the other yellow. There was a section at the back of the shop labelled "School Daze" and Jane crossed the thin synthetic carpet hopefully. The shelves were full of clumpy dark shoes with fat soles and chunky heels. She thought of her daughter's spindly legs and sighed. Abigail was now hobbling across the shop wearing red stilettoed boots. Her expression was one of stardom.

"Mind your ankle in those," said Jane, "And where is your coat? Oh!" She went and rescued the abandoned coat from a wire basket of plimsolls while Abigail selected some silver sandals.

"Come on Abi, I think we need to go to a different shop. Where are you own shoes?"

Abigail waved an indifferent hand towards the doorway and tentatively stood. Her feet slid to the front of the shoes. She teetered, knees bent and shoulders hunched, towards a mirror. Jane picked up the gaudy shoes she had tried on initially, returned them to the display stand and went to the doorway. There were several tubs of left shoes and a long stand announcing 'Cut Price Bargains' but no sign of Abigail's own shoes.

"Abi," she called," I can't see your shoes. Please come and find them."

Abigail lurched towards her.

"These would be great for a party. Oh..." Her expression froze as her eyes went to the empty spot where she had left her shoes.

"I'm sure I left them there."

For a second she looked frightened. Her dark eyes widened and her lips trembled as the realisation of a probable theft dawned on her. Jane thought she was about to cry. Instead she erupted into loud peals of giggles.

"They've gone!" she squealed, "I left them right there and someone's stolen them." She collapsed into a heap and shook with laughter. "Someone stole my smelly old shoes!"

The moment seemed rather less amusing to her mother.

"Abigail, it is not funny," she said.

"It is! It is!" laughed Abigail, tears streaming down her cheeks.

"Come along, we'd better find an assistant. Maybe someone has handed them in." This thought sobered Abigail sufficiently for her to follow her mother back into the shop. The shiny heels of the sandals dragged on the carpet and she concentrated on walking in a straight line.

The shop seemed rather lacking in sales assistants. Two bored young women lounged behind the counter. They were discussing their options for Friday evening, considering which clubs to visit and which friends to invite. One leaned sideways against the till, causing her dry blond hair to fall over her shoulder. She flicked it back with long pearly nails which were speckled with glitter. Her co-worker had frizzy brown hair and she was slightly too plump for the cropped top she had chosen to wear. Her pink flesh rolled across her low-slung jeans and a ruby coloured stone protruded from her navel. Their appearance did not inspire Jane with confidence.

She coughed.

"Excuse me," she began. Both assistants stopped talking and turned thickly mascarered eyes to glare at the interruption.

"My little girl left her shoes over there and they seem to have gone. Has anyone handed them in?" It sounded lame even to Jane's ears.

Abigail was scowling at the reference to "little girl" and the dark haired assistant had raised carefully plucked eye-brows, and was surveying the shop. One elderly lady was looking aghast at the price of fluffy slippers, and a pair of teenagers were browsing the handbags. Neither party looked especially public spirited.

"No," murmured the glossy lips, before adding, "Sorry." as an after-thought. She turned to continue her conversation.

"Oh," said Jane, defeated. She considered leaving her name in case they were handed in later but quickly decided that was both pointless and slightly ludicrous. She turned away.

"We'll have to buy these sandals then, wont we?" smiled Abigail.

"No," said Jane, summoning energy. "We'll find something cheaper and more sensible." She turned again to the flimsy displays and began to search.

#

Ten minutes later, they were heading towards a coffee shop. Abigail was wearing pink wellingtons and a resigned expression. They were still early enough for the precinct to be relatively empty and they quickly wound their way to a large department store. They walked past glossy leather handbags and pristine white rugs to the escalators. Jane could not imagine ever owning a white floor covering.

The coffee shop was situated on the first floor between the furniture department and children's fashions. Only someone who had never wielded a bulky pushchair with screaming occupant would ever place children's clothes on the first floor, thought Jane. She missed many things from when her children were babies, but not shopping.

She selected a damp plastic tray and peered through the glass barrier to see what delights the coffee shop had to tempt her with. There were glazed buns, dry pastry wheels and some rather glutinous gateaux slices. Some fat scones sat heavily in a basket next to thimbles of cream and tiny packets of jam.

"I think I'll just have a coffee," decided Jane. "What do you want Abi?"

"I'm starving!" she said, having spied an array of chocolate bars next to the till. "Can I have lemonade and some chocolate?"

"Please?" corrected Jane. She relented, "You don't deserve any after losing your shoes but yes, you can."

She paid the cashier and they moved to a table near the perimeter of the enclosure so they could watch the rest of the shop. Abigail unwrapped her chocolate and nibbled the caramel off the top.

"Eat that properly," said Jane, wiping a smudge of chocolate from her nose. She sipped her coffee. It was strong and delicious.

"Thank you God," she silently prayed. "I really needed this. Please help us buy Abi's school shoes, and if possible could we also find her old ones?"

Abigail was reading the menu card and wondering if they could come back for lunch. The puddings looked good. She looked out, over a sea of oak furniture and mountains of padded cushions, watching a young couple walk aimlessly through a display of coffee tables. Suddenly, she clutched Jane's arm, spilling her coffee.

"Mum! Look...."

"You spilt my coffee. What..?"

"My shoes," she hissed, "That girl is wearing my shoes."

Jane squinted to where Abigail was pointing, wishing she had worn her glasses. There was a young teenaged girl and she did appear to be wearing Abigail's shoes. They looked slightly small for her and her heels were squashing the backs. She wore ripped jeans and a faded jacket and carried a large blue carrier bag.

"They do look similar ...." began Jane doubtfully.

"They *are* mine," hissed Abigail urgently. "I recognise that sticker on the underneath of one. Look, you can see it when she walks. Quick mum, grab her. She's ruining the backs."

Jane half rose from her seat, unsure of her course of action. Then she sat again. The girl had been joined by a woman who Jane supposed was her mother. She resembled a sumo wrestler.

Dressed in a sleeveless vest that showed flabby arms, and an old skirt above stocky legs, the woman strode through the shop. Her short hair was matted, her eye-brows thick, and her mouth unpleasant.

"Wow, look at her," whispered Abigail. "She looks like a man dressed up as a woman. Do you think she'll hit you mum?" Her eyes shone in anticipation as she thought how interesting her news would be the following day at school. Not even Janine would have such a good story to tell. The same thought had occurred to Jane, though her response was somewhat different. She had turned away from the pair and was mopping coffee with a paper napkin.

"I think," she said nonchalantly, "that that poor girl looks like she needs those shoes and they were getting a bit small for you anyway."

"They're too small for *her*," persisted Abigail.

"Let's go, and I'll buy some sweets if you're good in the next shop."

They meandered through displays of pristine sports clothes and silk scarves, pausing to touch enticing fabrics. There was something irresistible about fluffy woollen shawls and languid satin throws, so they made many detours as they walked towards the exit. Abigail was keen to try on hats and had to be prised away from a stand of sunglasses.

Eventually they were back on the main street and Abigail tucked her hand into Jane's arm. They chatted about school and Abigail gave hilarious descriptions of the less attractive members of staff. Jane led her to a shoe shop known less for it's style, and more for it's thorough foot measuring regime and high prices.

Abigail sat obediently on a green plastic chair while a grey haired assistant moved the pink wellingtons to one side with distain, and began measuring her feet. In a short amount of time, Jane had bought a pair of extremely costly sensible shoes, and some jazzy socks to pacify her daughter.

There was time to buy lunch, but Jane was keen to leave. She told herself that she ought to collect Christopher fairly promptly, and that seeing Matthew was not a factor in her decision making, as they hurried towards the station.

Chapter Seven

As they walked towards the house Jane was pleased to see Mr Bobb's car was absent. She opened the door for Abigail then walked round the house to the back garden. Matthew looked up from a row of bricks and grinned. Jane noticed even teeth, and crinkled eyes that flashed at her. She smiled back.

"Have fun?" he asked.

"Not exactly," replied Jane and began to relay the morning's activities. As she spoke, Matthew slowly stood and put down his trowel, watching her while he listened. Unaccustomed to such an attentive audience, Jane found herself adding embellishments to make him chuckle. She rather liked making him laugh, she knew she was funny, and it was nice to be appreciated. He seemed amused, interested in what she was saying. He was noticing her, and she wasn't used to being noticed.

Matthew's eyes were green, she noticed and they sparkled when he laughed.

"Nothing as exciting has happened here," said the builder, when she finished. "We're just trying to get the first row of bricks down today."

"I'll make you some coffee," said Jane as she went towards the house. She could feel Matthew watching her as she moved away. It was not unpleasant.

#

In the kitchen, Abigail was holding the telephone, talking to Peter. Jane hovered for a while, then turned to fill the kettle. Abigail was giggling as she described the shopping trip to her father. After a few minutes of animated conversation she held out the receiver.

"He wants to talk to you now."

Jane picked up the warm telephone.

"Hi you," she said.

"Hello love. Sounds like you had an interesting shop. I can't talk for long, because I'm about to go to breakfast. Just checking everything's okay your end?"

"Yes," said Jane. She felt cross, pushed out again, and wondered how long he had chatted with Abigail before asking to speak to her. "We're all fine."

"Great, great. Well, I should be able to call again over the weekend. You can ring my mobile if anything comes up. I'm expecting a letter from work, it might be couriered, so you'll have to sign for it. Just leave it somewhere safe and I'll sort it when I get home."

There was a pause.

Jane felt she should say something meaningful or affectionate but the mood was wrong. It felt odd to be speaking midday to someone who had just woken up and the distance between them seemed tangible. She did not feel part of Peter when he was so far away and his call felt intrusive, breaking the flow of her activity. She resented the intrusion, resented that he was giving her a job, even though it would take her seconds to do. She felt like an employee, not a wife. Not someone who was interesting, funny, worth listening to.

"That's fine," she said at last. "Take care."

"Yep. Of course. You too. Love you." His voice was careful, detecting something was amiss but knowing he didn't have time for a drawn-out conversation.

"Bye," she said.

"Bye," he responded as she gently put down the receiver.

Jane turned back to the kettle and spooned coffee into two mugs. She felt unsettled by the call and as if she had failed in some way. It seemed wrong to not want to speak to your husband, but the dialogue had been unsatisfactory on many levels. She tried to imagine him in a hotel room, *wanting* to speak to her. But the image would not come to mind. The conversation had seemed primarily dutiful and it left her feeling empty. She remembered the excitement of hearing Peter's voice when they were younger, the intoxication of his mere presence.

#

Jane had been working in Marsden Unemployment office when she first met Peter. The building was a large red brick affair with an interior that smelt of old paper and disinfectant. The hard floors were grey and shiny and someone had decided that pale yellow walls would be a suitable match. Jane secured a job there on leaving school, only to discover (to her dismay) that many of the other employees had previously been teachers. They had abandoned their classes, but not their love of organising other people, nor their flair for sarcasm. There was a continual hum of authoritative voices speaking into telephones. Everyone shared the common belief that they could be doing something better with life, they were just not sure what.

Jane's first duty was mainly the mind-dulling, never-ending, filing of pieces of paper. Rooms lined with dark filing cabinets imprisoned her from nine to five each day. The harsh strip lighting and constant reading invariably sent her home at the end of the day with a headache. When she escaped each evening she found lucid thought an effort and walked like an automation to the bus stop. Jane hated work, but she needed the money and couldn't afford to leave.

She was soon elevated to the great responsibility of sending out pre-printed letters. She arrived each morning to a pile of buff coloured files and corresponding forms. Her task was to copy the name from the file onto a letter, copy the address onto an envelope and place both into a red plastic tray to await postage. It was slightly less monotonous than filing, but only just. Occasionally -

59

very occasionally - there was a spark of interest when she happened upon a name or address that she recognised.

"Why," wondered Jane,"would someone who lived in *that* road need to claim supplementary benefit?"

However, Jane had been promoted to the great heights of actually meeting claimants when Peter entered her life. It was summer time, and the office was particularly short of fresh air, with a surplus of smells. The windows were designed to stay shut, and instead the air (and smells) were stirred by fat white fans which sat precariously on various filing cabinets.

A long line of grey people had been directed to her cubicle, all bored, asserting their desire to work, their inability to find any. By the time they met Jane, they had succumbed to ennui and were devoid of all expression, their senses dulled by waiting in long lines in an enclosed space. Generally, she sympathised with them, though she did feel an amount of antipathy when handing over a cheque worth more than her monthly income to a suntanned father of three.

She had just checked the wall clock for the thousandth time, when she looked up to see a very tall youth smiling down at her. That in itself was odd. After standing in line for over an hour and being shuffled inexplicably into various seats, no one smiled when they finally reached the cubicle.

Worn jeans, clean but over-washed sweater, new training shoes, polite manners. He was obviously a student - these were still the days when unemployed students could claim benefits during the long summer break. He assured Jane he had been actively seeking work, then surprised her by enquiring if there were any jobs available at the benefit office. Initially, Jane assumed he was joking but as he then asked if she enjoyed her work and whether it was difficult, she decided his enquiry was genuine. She scuttled into a back room to find a supervisor who quickly whisked Peter into an informal interview lest he should change his mind. When he re-emerged he was the newly appointed, rather bemused, temporary filing clerk. He returned to Jane's cubicle from the other side of the desk and suggested that now they were work colleagues, she might meet him for a drink when the office closed.

She accepted the invitation with a smile.

They had sat in the sun next to a noisy road, nursing warm wine and talking. Jane found she could talk to Peter more than she had ever talked to anyone. He wasn't the glib operator she had first assumed, when she had accepted his invitation due to boredom. He was nice (an underrated word), and he listened. She could tell him about growing up with an elderly father and the muddle of guilt and relief when he died. She told him about her unusual, special mother, who somehow resembled a bright patchwork quilt, and how it felt to have no money, for anything, ever.

Peter was well-spoken and clever, with thick curly hair and very blue eyes. He lived in an intensely well ordered home with his parents and younger brother. His mother was severely efficient, and he found he enjoyed the relaxed randomness of Jane's mind. What had begun on an impulse, a sort of dare to himself, grew into a relationship. He felt protective when she made mistakes or lost things and he was amused by her muddles. She was funny, sweet, vulnerable - all the things his mother wasn't.

Their friendship developed quickly, deepening to a mutual dependency so that Jane found it inconceivable that they should ever part. It was not so much that she chose to spend the rest of her life with Peter, more that she could not imagine a life without him.

The relationship survived Peter's final year at university and he graduated and married during the same month. Jane never questioned why he had chosen her, never wondered at the disparity of their intellects or upbringing. She simply felt accepted by him, cared for, loved.

Looking back across the years Jane longed for those early months of married life. She sometimes thought of the seasons of her life in colours. The years as girlfriend then young wife and new mother were pink, sweet and pastel. Her childhood was yellow, bright and exciting when small, becoming pale and translucent as she neared the limpid years of adolescence.

"What colour am I now?" she pondered while wiping granules of instant coffee from the work surface. She thought of the complexities of a violent tinged horizon, heralding the close of one day and hinting at the weather to follow.

"Purple," she decided as she returned to the garden with coffee. "I am purple Jane."

The watchful green of Matthew's eyes followed her as she placed the coffee on a convenient window ledge. He rose to retrieve it and placed it on the fresh brickwork.

"Is that strong enough to put things on?" she said, wondering if the wet cement might seep out in protest at the additional weight.

"You'd be in trouble if it's not!" laughed Matthew, adding, "I wouldn't stand on it yet but I don't think a mug of coffee will do any harm."

Jane watched as he trowelled a fresh line of mortar over the bricks then carefully placed another block. She wondered if it was more difficult than it appeared but could not think of a way to ask if she could have a try.

"Lego for grown-ups," grinned Matthew, sipping his drink. "The worst part is humping supplies about and I seem to have lost my labourer to a protracted lunch break."

Jane was glad of the interlude and declined to comment. She had noted a freshly trampled rose bush and her dustbin was now splattered in cement. If the gauche builder chose to be absent she was not about to complain.

She crossed the garden to the forlorn bush, and tried to lift its misshapen branches. A spiteful thorn slid into her thumb joint and she gasped in irritation. The cut was small but deep. Matthew was standing, sipping his coffee, watching. He saw the dark blood trickle along her hand and moved to her side.

"That looks painful," he said. He reached out, taking her hand in his, turning it to examine the wound.

Her hand seemed tiny in comparison to his, and Jane felt small, protected. His touch was warm and surprisingly gentle, and she was suddenly more aware of him, of his closeness, than she was of the pain. She realised she was holding her breath.

"More annoying than anything," she said, forcing her voice to sound light, unconcerned.

His skin was rough, and he was holding her carefully, like she was made of glass. Like she was something precious. She withdrew her hand reluctantly.

"I had better find a plaster," she murmured, moving back to the house.

"Don't you drip blood on my bricks!" joked Matthew, watching her leave, with a bemused smile.

Chapter Eight

Friday morning dawned clear and bright. "Like an appetiser for summer," thought Jane, as she drove home from Christopher's playgroup. Yellow leaves were beginning to unfurl overhead and her mood reflected the few brazen daffodils that seemed to laugh at the hard soil as they stood proud and yellow against the dark earth. She had agreed to meet Suzie for coffee and she had just enough time to attack some housework but not long enough to be overwhelmed by it.

She parked and locked her car, cheerfully noticing Matthew's car and stoically registering Mr Bobb's, parked at an angle behind it. It resembled a car abandoned suddenly without thought, rather than one that had been carefully aligned with the curb and Jane was tempted to hope a passing vehicle might knock the wing mirror. She walked past the skip, which now had a bicycle perched precariously atop its contents and opened the front door. She went quickly to the kitchen, determined to present Mr Bobb with sustenance before he could ask for it.

The kettle had nearly begun to boil when there was a loud rap on the window, which nearly caused Jane to drop the mug in her hand. She looked up to the misshapen grin of Mr Bobb. He raised his hand to his mouth in a drinking gesture. Noticing Matthew behind the older man, watching her, Jane decided to feign ignorance. She raised her eye-brows and shrugged, conveying to Mr Bobb that she didn't understand. He began to pantomime with larger gestures, clasping his throat and rolling his eyes, while shouting, "A drink Janey, we need a drink!" She looked confused and frowned.

Matthew was laughing as he turned to continue his work. Victorious, Jane raised the purple mug to the window and Mr Bobb lifted a black nailed thumb to signal success. She made the coffee and tea, taking care to stir the excessive amount of sugar into the tea, then carried them outside and placed them on the ever growing brickwork.

"Thank you Jane," smiled Matthew.

"Thought I was destined to die of thirst today," shouted Mr Bobb. Jane slipped back to the house.

The debris from breakfast still covered the table and Jane began marshalling cereal packets into cupboards and sticky bowls to the sink. Max watched languorously from his basket. He flirted with the idea of raising his heavy body in the hope of attention but contented himself with the rhythmic thud of his tail.

Next on Jane's agenda were the bedrooms. She entered Abigail's room and followed a trail of dirty socks and discarded hairbands to the bed. With practiced speed Jane removed the bottom sheet and slipped the duvet from it's cover.

It was as she tugged the pillow free from it's case that she heard the music. It permeated the window and filled the room. Jane pressed her face to the cold glass and peered into the garden. The radio was on, exuding it's usual stream of slightly dated pop songs but today it was accompanied by live singing. Jane could hear Mr Bobb's voice, surprisingly tuneful and unsurprisingly loud, singing along to the music. Matthew's voice was very deep and full as he sang the love song. Jane sat back on the stripped bed and listened. There was something incongruous about the physical labour of building and the melodic soul of the ballad and Jane found it affecting.

The doorbell woke her from her reverie. Laden with laundry, Jane opened the door for Suzie.

"Ooh, who is singing?" asked her friend, "It's really nice!"

"You might want to check out appearances first," said Jane, beckoning Suzie inside. "I'll just dump these in the washing machine and then we can go."

The two women went into the kitchen and Suzie looked out of the window.

"Hmm, maybe not," she began as she saw Mr Bobb. Then her gaze rested on Matthew. "But he's not bad. Jane, you've been very quiet about him. Who is he?"

"I assume you mean Matthew," replied Jane, working hard to keep her voice nonchalant. "He seems nice. Too nice for sad married women. Come on, have you finished ogling my builders? Shall we go?"

"It might be more fun to stay here...." teased Suzie as she followed Jane to the front door. "Great body, nice face and a voice to die for! Does Peter know he's here?"

Jane laughed and pushed her friend through the doorway. "Behave," she said, collecting bag and jacket, and pulling the door shut behind her. She walked to the side gate and waved to Matthew.

"I'm going out," she called. Matthew rose and walked towards her.

"Okay, we've got our key, so it doesn't matter when you're back."

Jane looked up into his face and smiled. She felt Suzie at her back.

"Hello," said Suzie, keen to be noticed. "Looks like you've been busy." She looked around the garden, stopping when she saw the cement covered dustbin. "Oh dear, that's a mess. Will it wash off?"

Mr Bobb loomed, large and defensive, across the garden.

"Young Janey will clean that up in no time," he boomed, sounding militant. "You don't want to be paying me just to tidy up, now do you?

Jane smiled and pulled her friend away.

"Let's go before you cause any more trouble," she hissed.

"Janey?" said Suzie, "Since when have you ben called 'Janey'? You get in a strop if someone misspells your real name!"

"Since never," muttered Jane as she climbed into Suzie's car. "Trust me, not even Matthew is fair compensation for Mr Bobb."

Suzie drove a new but battered fiesta. Her doting older husband had finally put his foot down when choosing her a car and had refused to finance a more expensive model.

"You'll dent it within a month," he had correctly predicted. "Buy something I can repair cheaply."

It was not, as Suzie often explained, that she was a dangerous driver. Her mishaps were at very slow speeds and usually when parking or manoeuvring between obstacles. She had a tendency to hit stationary objects. There was, she had told Jane, nothing quite like the sound of metal scraping on brick to focus the attention.

She drove to the centre of town, not quite obeying any speed limits, and parked a short walk from the only decent coffee shop. As Jane opened the door the breeze disturbed the carpet of sweet wrappers at her feet and she stepped out carefully. They walked from the carpark to the main road and paused, waiting to cross. There was a fairly steady stream of traffic but this was something of a challenge for Suzie. She had perfected the technique of standing slightly forward and gazing directly at the driver. Before long a van slowed, flashing its lights to allow them to cross.

"Now can I have your phone number love?" called the driver.

Suzie laughed and waved. "You couldn't afford me," she said quietly, as she moved away.

#

The warm fug of the coffee shop, heavy with the dark aroma of coffee, greeted them as they entered the cafe. The tables were organised around the perimeter, with a large flower arrangement in the centre of the room. Oil paintings in bulky frames hung uncompromisingly on the walls, reflecting the solid wooden furniture. The bay window was swathed in heavy material that excluded much of the light, adding a cosiness to the atmosphere.

They moved to a table near the corner of the room and slid into the seats. A grey haired waitress hovered with raised eye-brows, ready to take their order.

"Are you a coffee Jane?" enquired Suzie. "Latte? Okay, two lattes please and I'll have a piece of chocolate brownie. Will you eat Jane?"

Jane felt somewhat flustered as she quickly scanned the menu card. She felt it was a little early for anything too sweet but also that she should order something to accompany her friend.

"A toasted tea-cake, please," she said, not really wanting to eat anything.

The silent waitress sighed, as though disappointed, and walked away on her sensible low-heeled black shoes. She was efficient, if unfriendly and returned within a few minutes with the correct order. She arranged crockery soundlessly on the polished surface, napkins, plates of food, mugs of coffee. Each item removed from her tray in strict order and placed before the women. She moved away and began to clear a vacated table, emitting loud sighs.

"Do you think she's the *ghost of the coffee shop* past, present or future?" whispered Suzie.

Jane giggled. "Definitely past. And I don't think she wants to be here any longer..." She sipped her coffee but it was too hot and burnt her lip so she replaced the china mug on its saucer. The knob of butter was melting on her tea-cake and she smeared it evenly with her knife. There was something wonderfully civilised, something intangibly British, about the coffee shop. She could imagine ladies from centuries past coming here, with long skirts and uncomfortable hats, discussing suffragettes and the place of women. Possibly served by the same waitress.

Suzie leaned back into her chair and inspected Jane's face.

"Come along then, do tell about your gorgeous builder and when exactly does your husband return?"

Jane smiled, "My builder is, I think, a good builder." She paused. She found she did not want to share the little knowledge that she did possess. If it was possible to create a secret where there was none, then Matthew was hers.

Peter was an easier subject, "Peter should return next week, though he wasn't sure of the day. Definitely before Easter weekend though because we have his parents coming."

"And has the enchanting Izzy gone with him?"

"I don't know, and I didn't ask." Jane's face clouded. Isabel Ainsworth was Peter's work colleague, and had been for the last two years. When she first joined the bank Peter had talked about her in great detail. He told Jane, perhaps unwisely, how talented Isabel was, what a great asset to the team and what a great sense of humour she possessed. He began quoting her at home, repeating quips she had said or interesting stories. When Jane objected, Peter had been annoyed. He said Jane was over-reacting and behaving like a jealous spouse when she had no cause.

"She's just a work associate," he had assured her, "I may like her and find her amusing but it's no different to if she was a man."

Jane thought it was very different. She knew that Peter worked alongside women and that the city had become the domain of many successful females. She realised that a good working relationship, irrespective of gender, was an essential part of Peter's job. However, she felt that beneath the mutual respect may be an undercurrent of interest that would not occur between two men. She disliked Peter being dependent on any female and was unhappy with the blossoming relationship. She wasn't sure if she was jealous, or simply wary.

Her worries were far from alleviated when she actually met Isabel. Peter had described her as "not pretty, plain looking."

However, Jane felt this was grossly inaccurate. Whilst Isabel was not perhaps pretty in a conventional sense, she had great poise and elegance, she would be described as a handsome woman. There was something classy about her, that spoke of old money, good manners, power. Her clothes were expensive, suits and scarves and silk blouses - clothes that Jane could never wear, even if she owned them, not with young children to care for. Isabel was also petite, with complicated blonde hair. Jane felt tall and gauche beside her and resented the baby fat that clung determinedly to her hips and stomach. Isabel was beyond competing with.

Jane had confided her fears to Suzie. Suzie had listened and tried to reassure her friend, especially as Peter's incessant tales of Isabel eventually dwindled to the occasional comment.

"He keeps coming home to you," said Suzie. "Besides, some men dislike too much sophistication in a woman...."

They had laughed together at that comment and it somehow helped to lessen Jane's worry. Now, when they met, Suzie would often demand an "Izzy progress report" and Jane found a delicious relief in venting her jealousy. As time passed her fears had softened to the odd niggle and Peter's constancy seemed dependable again.

Suzie cut her brownie into tiny pieces and began to stab them with her fork, eating them quickly. She adored chocolate and could consume vast quantities at any occasion. She realised this was alien to many women in their thirties, who considered sweet food exclusively for children and teenagers, having matured to more savoury tastes. Suzie felt she shared many feelings with teenagers, increasingly so as she neared her fortieth birthday. She was perhaps more self-aware than twenty years ago but many of her longings remained intact.

For a while, life had seemed so simple. The pursuit of career and then husband had been achievable goals, followed by intermittent years of waiting for a child. The birth of Tommy and subsequent sleepless days of continual care had been traumatic enough to preclude any serious thoughts on *Life* or what she wanted. She had been caught in the cosy web of early motherhood, entangled comfortingly with other women who shared her preoccupation with offspring. Her world had become very small, her only interests wrapped around her child.

But now she was beginning to emerge and look around once again at what the world might offer. Deep inside she harboured the tiny seeds of dissatisfaction. She did not know quite where she was aiming anymore and found the ever speeding passage of time alarming. She recognised the same concealed panic in other women her age. Women who had seemed contented homemakers suddenly launched new businesses or abandoned stable relationships for torrid love affairs. Suzie was quite sure she wished for neither, but she did feel a desperate need to do *something.*

She knew Jane well, was aware of a new restlessness in her friend. There was something not quite honest about their conversation, as if they were merely going through the motions whilst not actually sharing real feelings. She hoped her friend wasn't about to do something foolish. Whilst Suzie was merely an observer of midlife crisis at present, there was little evidence of happy conclusions to the love affair option, and the pain-ridden fallout was huge. However, she doubted if outside intervention would eliminate any danger, so she chose light banter not heavy discussion.

Hence the women sipped their coffee and chatted. They bemoaned the untidiness of their children and spouses, and the trauma of having to decide what to cook every day. Suzie regaled Jane with the story of her cousin's inability to keep a job.

"Honestly Jane, she's useless. I love her to bits, but she is the most impractical person I know. She finally managed to get a job, actually passed an interview, and started work - at the local library. But she even messed that up, I think she was there about a week."

"The library?" said Jane, "How can you mess that up? Did she talk too loudly or something?"

"No, not exactly," Suzie leaned forwards and lowered her voice. "She was asked to order some new books and then review them, and she decided it would be cheaper to buy them on the internet. Somehow she managed to buy some that were pornographic and illegal, goodness knows how she found them. Unfortunately, in her wisdom she put a couple on the shelf when they first arrived, thinking she was being efficient, and an old lady borrowed one and then complained to the library. Honestly! She's hopeless."

Jane shared her worries over the impending in-law visitation, and her inability to forget how sincerely her mother-in-law loathed her.

When they ran out of casual conversation, it was time to leave. Jane calculated their bill and they left the cash on the table as they rose to leave. The flippant talking had been fun, a necessary salve for their insecurities. Neither woman confessed that she was lonely, afraid of growing unattractive and unsure of her future. Their camaraderie was born of shared experiences and similar minds and too much personal disclosure would introduce an unnecessary strain on their friendship. They hurried back to the little car, watched suspiciously by the waitress who hurried over to count the money. Suzie drove to Jane's house.

"See you in a minute at playgroup," called Jane as she clambered from her seat. "Thanks for the chat, it was fun."

Suzie waved cheerily as she pulled away, and Jane turned to the house. She closed her eyes as she heard the welcoming bellow:

"Ah Janey, I expect you'll be putting that kettle on!"

Chapter Nine

Jane woke to the buzz of the alarm. She sightlessly reached out a heavy arm to quell the noise, annoyed she had forgotten to turn it off for the weekend. Warmly cocooned in the duvet, she prayed that Christopher would stay asleep.

The door inched open and a young voice said, "Was that the le'larm? Can I get up?"

"No," answered Jane, her voice thick with sleep.

Christopher stood poised in the doorway. This was not the answer he had been hoping for. He stood still, watching the hump that was his mother, then made his decision.

"I'll get in your bed then," he said, moving to the far side of the bed. "I 'spect you miss daddy."

He pulled back the cover, allowing a draught of cold air to reach Jane, then scrambled in beside her. He wriggled close, placing icy feet on her back.

"Stay on your own side and go to sleep," instructed Jane, still hoping that sleep might return.

Christopher shuffled. He pulled a pillow towards his stomach then pushed it back behind his head. He tried lying on his side, then his back, then his side. It was very difficult to get comfortable. Really, it was time to get up. He knew it was, he could hear birds singing and it had been light for hours and hours and hours. A bony elbow dug into Jane.

"Keep still," she snapped.

Christopher lay very still. He was on his back, arms at sides, legs straight out. He stared hard at the ceiling, determined not to blink and held his breath. He exhaled in a sudden rush, air and mucus exploding forth in desperation.

"Christopher!" said Jane, "It's like sleeping with an eel. Go back to your own room and put on a dressing gown. You can play quietly until I get up."

He climbed from the bed and bounced from the room, happy that permission had been granted. He could hear a car in the road as Mr James went to work, it was definitely time to get up. Perhaps everyone was ill. He started to hum *The Wheels on the Bus*, he liked that song.

"Quietly….." called Jane to his departing back.

Jane closed her eyes again, resigned to being awake for the day. Sounds of books being scattered filtered through the wall, and she knew that every minute she stayed in bed would be repaid in triplicate of tidying time. Reluctantly she rose.

It was to be a luxuriously empty day. Usually Saturdays were filled with ballet lessons and shopping trips, but there was nothing urgent and ballet would resume after Easter. Jane had a sudden longing for Peter. He had phoned the night before, his voice strong and familiar across the miles. His work was going well, he had assured Jane and he may be able to return on Wednesday. Jane had gone to bed missing him. The bed was very empty without him there. Jane wanted to feel the closeness of him again, to have his solidly warm body next to hers.

Jane dressed in a shapeless tracksuit and dragged her hair back with a fluorescent green hairband that Abigail had left on the bannister rail. She did not expect to see anyone all day so comfort took priority over pretty. She washed her face but left it bare of make-up and went downstairs.

Max wagged towards her, surprised and delighted that yet again she had arrived in the kitchen. He pushed his nose hard into her legs, then went in search of toys she might like to receive. He dropped a chewed sock at her feet as she reached for cereal boxes, and looked up beseechingly, eager for breakfast. Jane let him

74

briefly into the garden, then filled his bowl with dog food and put it on the discoloured mat next to his water bowl. He wandered back into the kitchen and began to crunch with enthusiasm.

Abigail and Christopher had appeared and were inspecting the cereal boxes. Jane passed them bowls and spoons, reaching to stop Christopher from pouring his own milk. She sliced bread and fed it into the toaster slots. No one spoke much, although Christopher seemed to be trying to make aeroplane noises. Jane collected plates and knives and began to butter toast while she ate a slice. She spread marmite onto Christopher's and cut it into triangles. He picked up a piece and began to suck off the salty taste.

"Eat it properly," said Jane, as she moved to open the door for the dog. Max pushed past her heavily and lumbered into the garden. He began to sniff the ground in earnest. Jane sighed and slipped her feet into Peter's slippers which had been left by the door. She grabbed a plastic bag and slopped into the garden to clear up dog mess from the previous night. So not her favourite job.

She found a trowel and walked across the wet grass wishing she had bothered to find some shoes. Disposing of dog mess was one of those elusive jobs that no one ever discussed and Jane was unsure of the correct procedure. It was like cleaning toilets or flossing teeth. One assumed there was a correct way to accomplish these things but if one had failed to notice during adolescence the intricacies of these tasks, there seemed to be no one to ask. They were not really subjects that naturally arose during coffee mornings or dinner parties.

Jane had devised a method of trowelling dog mess into plastic bags and disposing of it in the dustbin. She dimly recalled a half-forgotten clause in a council document concerning the disposal of excrement but could remember nothing useful. She did not feel inclined to call the council help-line on the topic.

Thus it was, this particular Saturday morning, a rather bedraggled Jane could be found, trowel in one hand, undesirable load in the other.....when the back gate swung open. Jane looked up into the handsome face of Matthew. *He* looked, she thought, like a freshly laundered shirt - clean from the shower, smelling of aftershave and soap, in a tee-shirt as green as his eyes. In contrast, Jane felt like a used handkerchief.

"Hi there," he greeted her, "I thought I'd get in an extra morning's work, if that's okay with you? It would be good to get the bricks to floor height and I can have the drain pipes delivered. Would that be alright?" He gazed at her, head on one side as her tried to gauge her mood.

Jane mustered a smile, very aware of the bag of poo in her hand.

"Yes, of course, that's fine." She deftly threw the trowel into a bush and held the plastic bag behind her back. Perhaps he hadn't noticed. "Would you like some coffee?"

"That would be great."

To Jane's consternation he began to follow her into the kitchen, leaving her in a quandary as to what to do with the poo.

"Do you have anything nice planned for today?" he said, trying to chat. It was Saturday, he didn't need to be here, and now Jane appeared distracted. He began to wonder if he'd made a mistake.

"No, not really," she answered, moving into the house and hoping the children would ignore what she was carrying. "We're just going to have a lazy day around the house."

Matthew was still following her. In desperation, Jane threw the bag into the kitchen bin. She would have to empty it as soon as possible. She walked nonchalantly to the sink and began to soap her hands, holding them under the flow of warm water.

"Hello Matt-few," said Christopher, "Do you want some rice-pops and toast?"

Matthew grinned, but didn't answer.

"You're welcome to some toast if you want some," offered Jane, pouring steaming water from the kettle into two mugs. She had forgotten to add coffee granules, so hurriedly poured it into the sink, added coffee powder then repeated the process.

"Well, I wouldn't say no, actually," said Matthew, watching her in amusement. "I don't usually eat breakfast but it does smell good. Are you sure you don't mind?"

Jane nodded, "Toast is the only thing I cook really well," she said.

"And sometimes she even burns that," snorted Abigail as she rose from the table. "You can sit here," she offered, gesturing towards her empty chair and pushing her plate to the centre of the table. "I'm going to watch telly."

Matthew hesitated, unsure of the protocol.

"Go ahead," said Jane, "I don't mind if you want to eat it in here; it would be nice to have some adult company for a few minutes."

She carried the coffee to the table and held the plate of toast towards Matthew. He took a slice and added a liberal coating of marmalade. Jane found she was no longer hungry and sipped her coffee. She was very aware of every tiny move and gesture that he made. She noticed the fine hairs on his arms as he rested them on the table and was struck again by how large his hands were. It felt strangely intimate to be sharing breakfast with a man, even with Christopher present. She wished she had taken more care when she dressed that morning, she felt old and plain next to him.

Matthew sat upright in his chair, enjoying the toast but not sure if he had crossed a line, if this was allowed. He didn't usually eat toast in his customer's kitchens.

Only Christopher was totally relaxed, and chattered happily to his new friend between, and sometimes during, mouthfuls of toast.

77

Gradually the builder began to ease back into his chair. He entertained Christopher with tales of his past cars, describing their colours and speeds to the eager child.

"What's your red car called?" he asked.

"An SLK," said Matthew, "and she's my best car yet, goes like like a dream."

He grinned across the table at Jane. "I had better go and do some work. Thanks for breakfast."

Jane rose and carried dirty plates to the sink. As she ran water over them she felt Matthew behind her and he reached around her to put his mug with the other crockery. Her body could feel where he made accidental contact at her shoulder, elbow and wrist. She forced herself not to lean back, against him, not to prolong the physical contact. She lowered her head, hoping he would not notice her raised colour or the unevenness of her breath. He paused, as though about to speak, then moved away. With a wave to Christopher he returned to the garden, leaving Jane alone with her fierce confusion.

Jane forced herself to continue with her day. She showered and redressed in casual jeans and sweater, taking time to apply make-up that wasn't noticeable - she didn't want to look like she'd tried - but also went some way to enhancing her eyes and detracting from her too large nose.

She heard a lorry arriving and looked outside to see a short square man delivering lengths of black pipe. His face was weathered and cross and his cropped ginger hair stuck up like the bristles on a scrubbing brush. He didn't seem to speak at all as Matthew helped him to unload, then he trudged back to his van and drove away. Neither man saw her watching.

Jane sorted out laundry, built a railway bridge with Christopher and searched dark dusty corners with Abigail, who had lost her library book. She waved at the postman, paid the milkman and collected discarded newspapers from around the house ready to be recycled. Exactly ninety minutes after breakfast, Jane allowed herself to make coffee and carry it outside.

The black pipes and guttering lay along the length of the garden. Matthew was busy at the side of the extension, listening to the radio as he worked. He thanked her as he rose to take the drink, then nodded at the radio and asked if it was bothering her.

"No, not at all," she reassured him, "Is that jazz music?"

He grinned. "Not a fan then? Yes, it's 'Jazz FM'. Mr Bobb isn't keen on decent music so I'm indulging myself in his absence." He settled back on an upturned box, happy to break from his labour. "Do you listen to music at all?" he asked.

"Well, only pop songs really and I can never remember who sings them." She looked at the cement encrusted old radio. "This is quite nice though. Makes you feel happy."

"That's partly why I like it. You can change your mood with music. It can relax you, and energise you. I love the freedom in jazz. There's no rules really, if it sounds good you can do it. The best musicians improvise much of the time. Bands tend to play together so often they can predict what each other are going to do. If you listen carefully it's almost as if they can read each other's mind, they finish each other's musical sentences. It's great. You have a great sense of belonging when you make music like that, it's like a communing of the spirit."

He stopped, aware he might be boring Jane, but she was smiling. It was nice listening to someone enthuse about something; most people seemed so apathetic about life.

"You should get Peter to take you to a jazz club," he said. "It's quite an experience the first time, you'd enjoy it I think."

Jane's smile weakened. "I don't think that's going to happen. We hardly ever go out now, he just works all the time."

"Well, I guess this house takes some paying for," said Matthew trying to sound reasonable, "and I suppose in his line of work you have to put in the hours to get on. You must get lonely sometimes though….

"Hey - look at those ants. I must've disturbed their nest and now they're moving house."

Jane knelt down where he pointed, glad of the distraction. She watched the industrious insects bearing their cargo of creamy eggs towards the flower bed, working together to save as many as they could. It excused her from responding to his comment and it was absorbing to watch the organised procession. It was interesting to watch the co-ordinated evacuation, the way they all worked together, each carrying their own load, independent, yet working for the common good of the colony.

For a while Jane and Matthew sat in companionable silence, sipping coffee and watching ants. He didn't seem in a hurry to return to work. The radio gave a news bulletin, and she listened to the reports of far off wars and political gossip.

"Half these politicians ought to be shot," said Matthew. "The whole country pays good money in tax and they seem incapable of making a decent decision. All they do is argue and score points off each other. If they spent the time listening and thinking, we might see a bit more wisdom and a lot less scandal."

"Yes, it does seem silly," said Jane, "that we know more about their private lives than their policies."

Matthew agreed, and they shared an amicable discussion on the wrongs in parliament. This extended to the problems in education and Jane shared examples from her wasted adolescence in school. He was amused by her stories and she enjoyed entertaining him. His laugh was strong and rich and it was unusual to receive so much positive attention. He listened to her - really listened, in a way that no one else did. Not anymore.

In turn, Matthew told anecdotes about his childhood. A household with four young boys was far removed from her quiet upbringing. She heard about their adventures making a tree house and their father's wrath when one brother relieved himself over a sibling below. His mother sounded securely capable and there was pride in his voice as he described her unruffled common sense.

He described how they had lived in a four storied town house with a long walled garden at the back. The area nearest to the kitchen had been used as a vegetable patch and Matthew had toiled beside his father on endless Saturday mornings, forcing the over worked soil to yield some sustenance. His father was fiercely proud of his produce and would extol the virtues of homegrown vegetables at every meal time. Matthew admitted to still feeling queasy whenever swede was served, which he had always hated but had been forced to eat. His father took it as a personal insult should any of his produce be rejected. He could recite word for word his father's lectures, on the cost of shop bought vegetables, and the amount of work involved in growing quality food at home, and how many nutrients were in the latter.

It was only recently that his mother had confided to Matthew that all was not as it appeared. Apparently, many of his father's offerings had been too puny for the family's huge appetite, or too insect ridden for her to want to deal with. So, unbeknown to her husband, she had slipped the vegetables straight into the bin and had instead served the family sanitised vegetables from the supermarket.

"Goodness knows what she did with the wrappers," laughed Matthew, "But I don't think Dad knows to this day what he was eating."

Jane laughed with him, and thought that she would like his mother very much. She could imagine the four boys, sitting together around a large oak table, kicking the shins of anyone who said something considered 'daft'. Matthew told her that they always ate dinner together and his father would select both wine and music to accompany each meal, and would carefully explain his choice to the family. Mealtimes had been filled with heated arguments and loud laughter; all accompanied by Elgar's or Mozart's music playing calmly in the background.

Jane wistfully considered this boisterous camaraderie, so alien to someone living with an ageing father and an eccentric doting mother. Matthew seemed so different, so secure and complete. While he spoke, his voice was warm, and Jane could tell he was recounting happy memories, that his childhood was a safe place he liked to remember.

Abigail brought the reminiscing to an abrupt halt. She flung open the back door to announce: "Christopher has finished watching his video and is spoiling my game."

Jane struggled to her feet.

"Sounds like my coffee break is over," she said.

"Maybe you'll be able to pop out later," suggested Matthew. "It's nice to have someone intelligent to chat to."

Jane gave him a searching look, unsure if there was hidden sarcasm in his statement. However, he held her gaze steadily with his own and the compliment seemed genuine. There was nothing flirtatious in his tone, though his expression was hard to fathom. As Jane walked back to the house she found herself grinning.

It was easy to find reasons to be in the kitchen for the rest of the morning. Jane set up the kitchen table with paints to amuse Christopher, then washed the cupboard doors. She emptied and wiped all the shelves, amazed at how many long forgotten tins lurked at the back. There were 'use by' dates that predated even Abigail. The bin needed emptying by the time she had finished, and she carried it, heavy and bulging, to her cement splattered dustbin.

Then she decided to hand wash some sweaters. This was indeed a rare event, as clothes were usually ruthlessly assigned to the washing machine and left to take their chances. However, today they were lovingly submerged in warm soapy water, the suds reaching up to caress Jane's elbows.

Not once did she glance out of the window or open the door, but she was ever aware of the proximity of the builder. As she rubbed the wool beneath the slippery water, her mind replayed their conversation. She dwelt on every nuance and expression, and heard again the deep tones of Matthew's voice.

She squeezed the clothes into fat sausages, watching the white foam ooze free and plop into the sink below. She remembered every word and gesture, and composed different responses for herself, reliving the conversation.

The water seeped quietly away and Jane swished clean water into the sink, the cold a shock to her skin as it sprayed her arms. She held the clothes under the flow and watched them swell with water then lazily rotated them in the bowl. In a rush she tipped away the water and placed the wrung garments on the draining board. It was time to plan lunch.

There was nothing worth eating in the fridge - nothing she could offer to a hungry builder should he choose to eat with them again anyway - so Jane hurried Christopher into the car and sped to the supermarket. Abigail elected to stay at home and read. Jane abandoned most of her list, buying just enough food to last until Monday. She did not ask herself *why* she was hurrying, but odd phrases from the morning's conversation were still replaying in her head. She thought about the words, over and over, like a story in her mind. She grinned when passing the shelves of neatly stacked vegetables, as though sharing a private joke.

On returning home, Jane was disappointed to find that Matthew was leaving.

"I'm off now, see you Monday," he said, handing her an empty cup.

"Oh. Right. Well, have a nice rest of weekend," she replied, the colour seeping from her day.

He grinned. "Thanks. You too, and thanks for breakfast. Bye..."

She watched him walk away, up the driveway, then busied herself with the shopping bags. She felt cross and dumped the flimsy plastic bags in a heap on the table. A lone tin of spaghetti hoops rolled out and onto the floor with a thump.

"Damn," muttered Jane as she retrieved the dented can. "Abi," she shouted. "You've watched enough telly for one day. Come and help me with this shopping and then we'll have lunch."

Abigail dawdled to the kitchen carrying a book, saw her mother's face and decided not to protest. Sometimes, she was learning, compliance was the easiest option.

Chapter Ten

The family meandered through the Sunday routine. Jane did not feel at all like going to church this week, but decided it was easier than occupying Christopher all morning. They arrived slightly earlier than usual and she decided to sit with Mr Beacham. He was an elderly gentleman who exuded both good humoured warmth, and the smell of peppermints. His watery eyes looked up at Jane's approach and he winked at Christopher. Beneath his thin grey suit he wore a patterned woollen waistcoat over a faded blue shirt. He had tucked a warm scarf over his chest but still managed to look cold. He held out a wrinkled hand to Jane and bid her good morning.

Christopher surveyed his neighbour from the safety of his mother's knee. He watched the yellow-tipped hands thumbing a worn Bible, then looked at the creased face. Mr Beacham was smiling at him in an encouraging manner and the boy felt emboldened to speak.

"Are you very old?" he whispered.

Shocked, Jane was about to intervene when to her horror she heard him add: "will you die soon do you think?"

"Christopher!" she said, "That is very rude."

Deeply embarrassed she looked at the old man. Mr Beacham patted her hand and his eyes narrowed in laughter.

"Ha!" he exclaimed. "No one else has dared to ask me that, though I'm sure my son would like to know. He grinned at Christopher. "Not today I hope."

Jane was relieved to see the deacons and pastor walk to the front of the church. With a rousing first hymn, the service began.

Jane found it hard to concentrate during the sermon. Her thoughts returned time and again to Matthew and whether or not she would have a chance to chat with him the following day. She rehearsed conversations in her mind, but found when it was time for prayer, to talk to God, she had nothing to say. When the service ended, feeling strangely empty, she had a few meaningless conversations with friends before collecting her children and departing.

Pastor Rob watched her leave.

"I think," he said later, to his wife, "that Jane Woods is rather lonely." Esther, who was much too busy to even think about being lonely, declined to comment.

#

Jane awoke late on Monday. She lay still for a while, listening to the dual sounds of one of Christopher's films and the cement mixer outside. She had slept heavily due to the greater part of a bottle of red wine and now her head, whilst not exactly hurting, had a thick dryness inside. She walked heavily to the shower.

Abigail and Christopher were contentedly perched in front of the television. Abigail had helpfully "done breakfast" which consisted of dry cereal, straight from the packet and cartons of chocolate milk. Jane threw away empty cartons and sticky straws, and wiped the table before moving to the kettle. She jumped when Mr Bobb thumped loudly on the window. She bared her teeth and held up the kettle, saw his raised thumb in the corner of her eye, and settled to making coffee. The attraction of Matthew was heavily diluted by the presence of Mr Bobb.

On looking into the garden, Jane was surprised to see absolutely everything was covered in a fine pink dust. Mr Bobb, resembling a monstrous marshmallow, was wielding a powerful machine that was cutting through bricks where the extension would join the existing house. The noise was tremendous and when Jane opened the kitchen door, plumes of airborne dust clouded inside and settled on every surface. She hurriedly shut the door again and took the workers their drinks via the front of the house. Even as she walked towards them, the dust formed in a film on the surface of the mugs, and she could feel the suffocating powder in her nose and mouth. Mr Bobb turned off the machine when he saw her.

"Hello young Janey. Hope we didn't wake you," he shouted full of glee, obviously enjoying the power of his brick cutter. Perhaps because it was so noisy. And created so much mess.

He took a great swallow of tea, undeterred by its speckled surface.

"Taking this tool back to the hire shop soon, then I'm off to another job. Got to keep the work coming in you know. Matthew will be here all week and I'll come if he needs help. Might send young Kev round for a bit. We don't just abandon jobs half way through like most builders; don't you worry."

Jane tried not to look too pleased at this news as she gazed at her pink coated garden.

"You need a spot of rain to clear this up," said Mr Bobb, watching her. "And you want to sweep up a bit when I've gone or you'll get it tracked into the house. It won't take you a minute, and after all, you don't want to be paying me just to clean up now, do you?"

Jane smiled, nodded and returned to the house.

She played with her children and found things to clean and tidy until she heard the high revs of Mr Bobb's car leaving. She then combed her hair, checked her make-up and wandered into the garden to find a broom.

Matthew looked up as she approached, and stopped working.

"He always looks so pleased to see me," thought Jane as she pulled the old broom from the shed.

As she swept, they shouted comments about the weather and the news. Then Jane stopped sweeping - she seemed to be mostly just rearranging the dust anyway. She leant on the broom while they discussed his holiday plans. She watched him talking, noticing the pink tinge to his hair, wanting to reach up and brush it out for him. After half an hour, Jane rested the broom against the wall and returned to the house and Matthew continued building.

The next two days passed pleasantly. The children were glad to stay comfortably at home and took advantage of Jane's slight absence of attention to watch rather more television, and to eat many more biscuits, than was generally allowed. Jane pottered about the house, going outside at regular intervals to talk to Matthew. The builder, in response, began to appear in the kitchen under the pretext of returning empty mugs. He would then lounge against the kitchen cupboards watching Jane work while amusing her with tales from his past, or comments on life in general. Conversation was never awkward. She began to feel that she knew him better than some of her closest friends. In return, she spoke at length about her childhood, telling him details that she rarely shared with others.

Jane's father had been aged sixty when she was born. He was thirty-five years older than her mother. She had often wondered why they had married and concluded that her mother was intent on escaping the insecurities of a travelling family and this was her first chance.

Jane knew very little about her grandparents and had only ever met them once, squashing into an overheated mobile home (which was no longer mobile) and sitting on a shiny sofa. It was very shiny, as it was still covered with the protective plastic from when it was new. The house wasn't unpleasant, and was very clean, with a tiny white fence around the outside and flowers growing. It seemed to her like a nice place to live, almost a toy house.

Then she heard the people next door shouting, and listened to her grandmother complaining about the cold, and the rain, and realised that there wasn't a separate room she go into to escape the adult conversation, as every sound seeped through the partition walls. Even sounds when someone used the toilet.

She knew that her grandfather had been an artist and a drunk and that her mother was keen to leave him in the past. Jane imagined that her own father had seemed very gallant and protective to the young Daphne.

When Jane was two, her father had a stroke which left him paralysed down his left side. His mouth drooped, making articulation difficult and he walked with a stick. Daphne remained devoted to him.

Some of Jane's earliest memories were of her father, always dressed in a blue shirt with the top button undone, watching television. He had the volume turned too high for comfort and he invariably watched horse racing. Racing was his passion and Jane was still only vaguely aware of how much money had been squandered on bets. The walls of the sitting room were lined with photographs of horses jumping fences, the jockey's colours bright behind the glass.

Jane remembered rugs on the floor littered with an array of footstools and poofs. The dusty windowsill was jammed with cacti. Next to racing, her father loved cacti. They were not pretty to Jane's eye, who longed for delicate leaves and petite flowers to enter the home. Their gnarled old stalks stood defiantly in their pots. Every so often, one would fling forth a flower, large and clumsy and at odds with the plant that had produced it. Jane hated them and would have damaged them had their spikes not protected them.

When Jane grew older, she began to be embarrassed by her father. Visiting friends often assumed he was her grandfather, and she did not always correct them. She watched other children playing with their fathers, being carried by them or running away to be chased. She felt that her father had failed her.

He died when Jane was ten. A second stroke was too much for his weakened body. Jane missed him. She missed the tickle of his chin when he kissed her and his chuckles of delight when she told him about school. She missed the look of pride in his eyes when she did something well and the comforting, musty smell, when she snuggled beside him on the sofa.

Everyone expected Daphne to be distraught and maybe in the privacy of her room she was. However, to the outside world she showed a quiet dignity as she sorted her affairs, calculated what little money remained and moved into a flat with her daughter. She remained determinedly independent, finding a job as a florist and supporting Jane as she developed into adulthood.

"She's always been my best friend," Jane confided to Matthew. "You see, I've always known that she needed me, as much as I needed her. And she's always given me space. I could do anything and I don't think she would judge me."

"Anything?" said Matthew.

"Well, maybe not quite anything..." admitted Jane.

#

Late Wednesday morning Peter returned home.

Jane heard the taxi pull up outside and went to open the door. Christopher and Abigail jostled for position, waiting impatiently while he paid the driver and retrieved his cases from the boot. They rushed towards him as he walked down the path and he picked them both up in a giant bear hug.

"Daddy, daddy, daddy," sang Christopher.

"Have you got us presents?" asked Abigail.

"Yes, of course," said Peter as he staggered to the front door and deposited them on the doorstep. His eyes met Jane's and he leant towards her.

"Hello love, I'm home."

She led the family to the kitchen and offered him a drink.

"No thanks, I ate pretty well on the flight. I do need a kiss though, come here."

He held her tightly so she could hardly breathe. She smelt the stale aeroplane air, the smell of uncleaned teeth, and felt the rough stubble of his unshaven chin.

She pulled away, asking, "Did you miss me?"

She saw surprise register in his eyes.

"Miss you? Well, yes, I suppose. I was too busy working to miss anyone much. I did miss you at night though," he added, gazing at her with bright eyes laden with meaning.

"And I have presents!" he announced, his tone lightening.

It was not the response Jane had wanted. Not the response she felt she needed, deserved. But she said nothing

The two children heaved his case into the kitchen and waited expectantly. The dog, realising some event was taking place, plodded over and presented Peter with a sodden slipper. Peter patted him absently while unfastening the case. Wads of dirty socks and crumpled shirts exploded out onto the kitchen floor.

"Mummy first," directed Peter. He passed Jane a satin covered chocolate box and the latest novel by a favourite author.

"Love you," he said as she took them. "Now, down to business…."

Both children were given sweatshirts and Jane was surprised to note he had bought the correct sizes. There was a much longed for CD for Abigail, and a book about tractors for Christopher. He also gave them both the inflight travel bags he had received on the planes. Christopher spent a happy ten minutes pulling on socks up to his thighs and wearing ear-plugs and eye-shades. Abigail was more interested in the lip-gloss and peppermints.

"How's the extension coming on?" asked Peter, moving towards the door. "I'll just pop out and have a word with Matthew. You getting on with him okay?"

Jane was careful to keep her voice neutral as she replied, "Oh, he seems pleasant enough.

"Will you eat lunch with us?" she asked, keen to move the conversation on.

"Well, I wont eat much," called Peter as he left the kitchen, "but I will come and sit with you."

They had an amicable lunch, despite Peter's brain being rather fuzzy after a night flight. Jane found there were several seconds of delay between her questions and his responses, as his tired brain struggled to process information.

He spent the afternoon on the telephone working, and playing rather half-heartedly with the children. During his phone call Jane took a drink out to Matthew but she did not linger. It was not, she reasoned, that there was anything wrong with the time she had spent chatting to him but she instinctively felt that Peter would disapprove and it was not a discussion she wanted to have. No point in looking for trouble where there wasn't any.

Chapter 11

The building was progressing steadily. The new floors had been flooded with thick grey cement and Jane had resisted a childish urge to carve her initials into the glutinous mass. The bricks were now rising towards window height and Peter had been pleased when he saw them, with the colour match as they interlocked with the house.

"That's why Mr Bobb is worth having Jane," he had assured her, "Tom said he would be careful over details."

The following morning Peter went to work as usual.

"Real men don't get jet-lag." he rather grumpily informed Jane as he peered at her through red rimmed eyes. "I know it's Good Friday tomorrow, but I may work anyway so I can catch up before the long weekend."

Jane found she did not want to argue with him and he was rather disappointed by her lack of persuasive effort. He looked across at her as she combed her hair. There was something different about her, something he couldn't quite put his finger on. But he didn't have time to think about it, he needed to leave for work.

When Matthew arrived, Jane met him with coffee and a smile. He told her that Kevin would be arriving later that day to help with the labouring. They talked about nothing of importance for a while and then Jane collected her children and shopping list and headed for the supermarket.

The list was long and intended to provide food for the whole of the Easter weekend. Abigail read it aloud in the back of the car while Christopher contentedly chewed the edge of his seat belt. He watched a line of dribble run down the belt, past his shoulder and almost to his elbow. He glanced furtively at the rear view mirror to see if Jane had noticed. She had not, so he surreptitiously added another blob of spittle.

While managing to respond appropriately to Abigail's chatter, Jane's mind was replaying her conversation with Matthew. She was remembering how his teeth seemed very white when he smiled, and she relived the sentences that had made her laugh.

They arrived at the supermarket without Jane really being aware how they had got there. She assumed she must have stopped at any red lights and checked properly at junctions but she really could not remember. With an effort, she dragged her mind back to the present and went to select a shopping trolley.

The shop was full. Jane plonked Christopher into the child seat of the trolley, ignoring Abigail's, "He's too old for that," and negotiated her way around a stack of bread and into the heart of the store. She squeezed past a man who was standing, hands in jeans pockets, staring in bewilderment at an array of plastic wrapped apples. Deftly collecting fruit and vegetables Jane continued to the weighing station.

"Can we buy strawberries?" pleaded Abigail.

"No, too expensive," said Jane.

Two young boys were playing with the scales. They had printed an assortment of price stickers for different vegetables, though only a potato was on the scale. They moved away as Jane approached and she saw one stealthily stick *pickling onion* onto the back of an unsuspecting old lady. They dissolved into helpless giggles as the woman moved away and Jane found herself wanting to laugh.

The family advanced to the meat aisle and Jane selected sausages and chicken mince.

"Can we have burgers?" pleaded Abigail.

Next on the list were cans of soup and baked beans. Jane manoeuvred the wayward trolley past two women who were complaining loudly about the parking. One had a *turnip* sticker on her back.

"Why do I always choose the trolley that wants to keep tuning left?" moaned Jane, narrowly missing the shins of a green clad assistant.

"Can we have baked beans with sausages in?" pleaded Abigail.

"No."

They found milk, cheese and butter.

"I'm cold! I'm cold!" said Christopher, shivering, as they passed the fridges.

"Can I have chocolate mousse?" pleaded Abigail.

"No, help me to find the cream," said Jane.

They followed a suited gentleman walking extremely slowly towards the pet food section. He had a slight limp and his back bore a *parsnip* sticker. They found the shelf holding the only food her cat would deign to eat, and Jane surveyed the flavours. *Turkey, chicken, salmon, lamb.* Jane wondered what incentive drove people to buy for their animals, food that humans would choose to eat. Why not *mouse, sparrow* and *spider* flavours? she thought. It was after all, what her cat would choose to eat.

They continued past rows of enticing biscuits and sweets, and a depleted arrangement of Easter eggs.

"Please can we buy some sweets?" pleaded Abigail.

After selecting pre-sliced bread and an apple pie - where Abigail pleaded for ginger cake - they came to the cleaning materials. Jane dumped toilet rolls, bleach and washing liquid into the trolley. She referred to the list as a very tall lady swept gracefully past. She wore high heeled boots and carried a basket brimming with organic produce. She had an *asparagus* sticker on her back.

Jane seemed to have already passed much of what she needed. She sent Abigail in search of eggs, and swung the trolley round to retrace her steps.

By the time they had finished, the trolley was stacked high. Steering took great effort as they headed towards the check-outs.

"Can we have nice cereal?"

"Can we buy wafer biscuits?"

"Can we have cheesecake?"

Jane ignored Abigail and looked in dismay at the queues of customers waiting to pay. Only four tills were operating and several laden people stood patiently waiting at each one. Jane selected at random a middle line, and forced her shopping cart into place.

"I need the toilet," announced Christopher. "Right now."

Jane knew better than to delay. She left Abigail with strict instructions to reserve their place, and went in search of washrooms.

On their return, she saw they had nearly reached the front of the queue. Abigail was flinging misshapen bread and partly thawed ice-cream onto the moving belt.

"Excuse me," frowned the shop assistant, looking at Jane, "Is this your shopping?"

"Yes," said Jane.

"Well, this is an express till. You can't bring a trolley in here."

"Oh," said Jane, somewhat flummoxed, "I'm sorry, I didn't see the sign."

The girl pointed an abnormally long orange finger nail above her head.

"Baskets Only" declared the sign. People watching began to sigh and tut.

"Really?" said Jane. "I'm very sorry, but you see, I hadn't noticed. It will take us longer to move our stuff than for you to just scan it…."

But the checkout girl was shaking her head. "Not allowed to do that. Baskets only. There's people waiting."

"Typical," the woman behind said, though she had not thought to point out the sign to the hapless family earlier, "no consideration for other people."

Red faced, Jane began to reload the trolley. "It doesn't matter," she hissed to Abigail, who looked close to tears, "it was just a mistake."

"People are watching us," said Abigail, helping her mother to scoop shopping off the belt.

"It doesn't matter," repeated Jane. "Here, buy some chocolate to cheer yourself up."

They moved awkwardly to the back of the next line. Jane would have abandoned the shopping and left, but they needed the food. After an eternity they managed to pay for their groceries and return to the car.

"That was *so* embarrassing," declared Abigail, as Jane reversed out of the space. "I am never coming to this shop again."

Jane shared her feelings as she drove carefully towards the exit. She saw another mother struggling to control excited twins, and an old man carrying a single bag of shopping. As they neared the exit barrier Jane noticed an elderly woman heaving bulging bags into the boot of a shiny Mercedes. Stuck to her red coat was a label and Jane could just make out the word *beetroot*. She smiled, and drove home.

#

As Jane turned into her street she was met by a large truck bearing an overflowing skip. Particles of dust showered her car as it passed her and in her mirror she recognised the bath tub wobbling

97

precariously on top. She hoped it was more secure than it appeared to be.

When home, she parked in her now vacant driveway. Matthew came out to greet her and as she opened the boot he leant inside to lift out the shopping.

"I'll give you a hand with these," he offered. "Did you pass the skip? You just missed it."

"Yes," replied Jane, who was hoping Matthew had not selected bags containing any personal hygiene items. She led the way into the kitchen, pleased to notice the children had followed Matthew's example and were also laden with bags.

"Can I put the kettle on?" asked Matthew.

"Of course," smiled Jane, elbows deep in the freezer as she fought with peas and chips to make space. "You could make one for me too, if you like," she suggested, forcing chicken nuggets between two tubs of ice-cream. A frozen plum rolled defiantly to the front.

Jane had been presented with a bag of homegrown plums every year for the past three years. She hated plums, but could not think of a way to avoid them and did not want to offend the generous friend. Each year the fresh offering replaced the previous one, which was deposited in the rubbish. Now the plastic bag had split, and the rock-like fruit had rolled to each corner of the freezer. One day she would unload everything and throw away the solid balls of citrus ice.

She removed a pizza from its box so that it would fit, then closed the freezer door with emphasis.

She looked up to see the builder laughing at her. He stood, feet crossed, leaning against the sink.

"Do you think your freezer skills reflect your general organisational abilities?" he said.

"I think," said Jane," that if you are rude to me, I will fire you."

He passed her a coffee and she sat at the table and surveyed the mess of shopping.

"I hate putting shopping away," she confided. "It takes so much effort to buy it all and there never seems to be any space at home to put it all away properly."

"Not a problem when you're shopping for one," said Matthew, "My flat is the epitome of tidiness."

Jane looked at the clock. She could steal a few minutes before she began the next mundane activity. She relaxed into the chair, settling for a chat. She loved talking to Matthew. She felt like a child having an imaginary friend. He was so far removed from her life and her social group, that she was confident he would never repeat what she told him. So she spoke with the abandon usually reserved for the very old or very young. She was honest about her feelings on issues, and her frustrations at the tedium in her life. There was safety in the social difference between them, because even if he chose to share her secrets, who would he tell? None of his friends would be interested in a woman they had never met. His temporary status in her world was also a comfort as it was unlikely they would ever meet when the work was completed, lending the friendship almost the intensity of a holiday romance. Not that she'd ever had one.

She found herself talking about Peter, things he hated, the impact of his job, the faults that irritated her. It was a rebellion against all those suppressed emotions that float aimlessly inside everyone but are rarely expressed. She was particularly free in her remarks about Hilary. Matthew stood and listened with amusement to her cruel descriptions of her mother in law. Every so often he would gaze at her with his intent, green eyes, causing her to wonder at the thoughts behind them. Did he enjoy her company or was she just an excuse to not work? Did he *like* her? It was beginning to matter.

99

Jane thought about Matthew constantly, even when he had packed up and gone home for the day. She composed stories to tell him, savouring details she thought he would enjoy. She began to watch her own life as though through the eyes of a third person; and it was gradually slipping from her grasp, becoming less real and less important. She rehearsed conversations over and over in her mind, imagining responses. Her interactions with him became the most important part of her day and when he was gone, she remembered every gesture and tone, and the most fleeting of expressions.

She never questioned her growing obsession or wondered where it might lead. Later, she would be unable to differentiate exactly at which point the friendship became something more, at which point her feelings began to dominate her good sense. She would never know when something good became harmful. But that was for later, back then, as she prepared for Easter, she thought everything was fine. It seemed both harmless and exciting, and she felt like the main actress in an acclaimed performance. It left her warm and happy. She was very happy. How could that be anything other than good?

#

Easter Saturday began with a rainstorm. Jane lay in bed and listened to the rain pelting against the window. She felt cold and slid closer to Peter. He was always warm. It was the thing she missed most when he was away, and now she snuggled against his shoulder, enjoying the feel of him. He looked like Christopher when he was asleep. They shared the same fine bone structure and long straight nose.

Jane was dreading today almost as much as Sunday. Today she must marshall the house into some semblance of order and clean in places usually ignored. She also felt vaguely guilty about yesterday. Peter had gone to work as forewarned, albeit for a shorter day than usual. Jane had spent the day at home, mainly talking to Matthew.

Her guilt arose from her lack of church attendance. Usually she would have taken the children to the special Good Friday service, where the children would make Easter crafts and be taught the Bible story, while the adults contemplated what the death of Christ had bought for them. It was a service that Jane enjoyed. Devoid of the superficial glitter that tended to distract from Christmas services, Easter was very real. The deep truths of pain and death, mingling with forgiveness and freedom were poignantly real to Jane.

However, this year some inner obstacle stopped her from wanting to attend. She could not define why, she simply did not want to sit and spend long minutes thinking about a holy God. It was easier to not think.

Beside her, Peter stretched and turned a sleepy head to look at her. He yawned and rubbed his nose.

"Did the rain wake you? Sounds awful out there! Hope it wont ruin those window frames they put in yesterday."

"No," Jane reassured him. "The builder knew it might be stormy today and he said everything would be fine."

She had watched Matthew pack away his tools for the weekend, securing plastic sheeting over mountains of sand. He told her he would spend Easter with his parents and she had guessed he was looking forward to it.

He had been assisted during the afternoon by Kevin. Kevin was a rather shy teenager with a fantastic body and appalling skin. His acned complexion flushed scarlet whenever Jane approached and he consumed vast quantities of cola. This might account for his teeth which were large and grey and too numerous for his mouth. He had a mass of curly brown hair that Jane honestly doubted had ever been brushed. He also possessed black eyes and she could feel him watching her, cat like, whenever she ventured into the garden. He worked steadily, whistling tunelessly through his protruding incisors as he carried great weights of bricks and stacked them ready for Matthew to lay. When it was time to leave he waved awkwardly through the kitchen window before chugging away on his scooter.

"Simple, but bloody strong," stated Matthew.

"And a lot less annoying than Mr Bobb," thought Jane.

#

The day did not turn out to be as torturous as expected. Peter guessed that Jane would be thrown into a spasm of cleaning by his parent's visit, so preempted some of the stress by promising Abigail vast amount of money if she helped. Dreaming of nail polish and chocolate, the child decided to oblige. So while Jane scrubbed toilets and vacuumed floors, Abigail wiped finger marks from doors and carried abandoned garments to their correct rooms.

Christopher was commissioned to tidy his bedroom. However, when Jane happened to open his door she found he had been unable to resist the attraction of long lost toys from under the bed. He sat cross legged surrounded by an assortment of dusty toys and random puzzle pieces, which he had somehow connected to create a misshapen masterpiece. Jane quietly left him to play. Him being safely occupied was probably the greatest help of all.

She returned to the kitchen to prepare vegetables. Abigail was busy at the table with an empty yogurt pot, string and aluminium foil, which kept tearing.

"I saw this on telly," she explained. "It will be a pretty vase for the table. Except their glue didn't dry up and their paper didn't tear."

She wound lengths of string around the top of the container and held it stickily in place. When she tried to remove her fingers, the string clung on, refusing to adhere to the pot.

"I can't do it! Stupid thing," she spat in frustration, "why wont it stick?"

"Shall I help?" said Jane, leaving the potatoes in a murky sink of water. "Maybe if we tape it in place?"

"No, they didn't use tape," said the angry girl, determined to make an exact replica of the receptacle demonstrated on the programme.

"I expect they did, they just didn't film that bit," said Jane, as she attached the string firmly with tiny pieces of tape. "We can take it off when it's dry if you like but I think it looks very nice. Grandma will think it's lovely."

Abigail surveyed her handiwork with a critical eye.

"S'pose it's okay," she conceded begrudgingly.

Jane returned to her vegetables with a wry smile. It was, she reflected, a mixed blessing when children decided to be helpful.

Abigail left the kitchen in search of spring flowers. Jane doubted if she planned to return to clear away her materials and mentally added it to her list of jobs. Her mind wandered to Matthew. She wondered if he had reached his parent's house and was now lounging in his mother's kitchen as he had in hers. Would he think of her at all today? She thought not and somewhat wistfully took the potato peelings outside to compost. The garden seemed empty without him and she did not linger to help Abigail pick flowers.

Chapter Twelve

Easter Sunday dawned grey and damp. The children woke early, eager for chocolate eggs and Jane heard them whispering noisily outside her door. Peter was gone, she guessed to make tea and she clung fretfully to the pillow. She had hoped vainly for a blizzard last night or to wake with a fever and be confined to her bed. However, it seemed today was destined to happen and she must endeavour to survive. She rubbed her eyes, noticing that her hands were scented with pine, absorbed when cleaning the sinks the previous day. Not quite the perfume she'd been hoping for.

Breakfast was a non event. The children's eyes were full of gaudily-wrapped chocolate in over-sized packaging, and after a few forced mouthfuls of nutrition Jane relented and let them indulge. Why not? They weren't going to eat anything worth eating anyway.

She watched as Christopher struggled to force the egg from its box, and then quickly removed the coloured foil. The egg split in two and he held one half to his mouth, covering his face and savouring the warm chocolate smell as he bit into the egg. Smudges of brown coated his nose and cheeks as he chewed contentedly. Abigail was more tentative. She sought to preserve the patterned card as she carefully unfolded it to release the egg. She peeled back a tiny corner of wrapper and snapped off a portion of chocolate to suck, before rewrapping the egg so it appeared complete.

Jane felt slightly queasy as she forced herself to decide when to start cooking. She had a physical aversion to planning anything and the thought of coordinating an efficient lunch made her muscles stiffen and her head ache. She hated cooking, really hated it. Cooking for her parent's in-law was even worse.

"Why are you frowning?" asked Abigail observing her with keen eyes. She was wary of her mother's moods, and liked to know what caused them. "Do you want some chocolate?"

"No, thank you," Jane mustered a small smile. "Daddy gave me my own egg this year. It's very pretty and very big. No, I was thinking about dinner, that's all. I think Grandma will arrive about 12 o'clock, so I should put the turkey roll in about 11:30." She frowned again, wondering if she would remember to preheat the oven.

Bored, Abigail collected her egg and slid from the room.

"I wouldn't go in there," she advised her father in the hall. "She'll give you a job."

Peter raised his eyebrows and opened the kitchen door. Jane was peering crossly at the bowl of potatoes she had peeled the previous day. The top ones had protruded above the surface of the water and were speckled with black spots. The starchy water felt slimy as Jane tried to force them further down. She wondered if she ought to cut off the blackened edges but she had no new ones to replace them with. There wouldn't be enough if she made them all smaller and threw away the black bits.

"Maybe," she decided, "If I roast them really well, no one will notice. I'll make sure the top ones are extra crunchy."

"I've put the books in order for you."

Jane looked up in confusion. "Books?" she said.

"Yes, books in the study. I've dusted them all and put them in alphabetical order. Anything else you want me to do?" He sat contentedly at the table and smiled helpfully.

Jane, lost for words she dared use in front of a child, said nothing.

Max lovingly placed a chewed bone on his knee and gazed up in adoration. Peter fondled his silky ear then reached for Christopher's chocolate.

"Enough of that for now," he said, as the boy began to protest. "You shouldn't be allowed to eat it for breakfast anyway."

Jane bristled at the implied criticism and poured fresh water over the souring potatoes. Peter reached above her and put the opened chocolate in a cupboard.

"It will go stale if you leave it like that," thought Jane, not bothering to speak. She tipped the potatoes into a saucepan and water splashed out, puddling the work surface and wetting her sleeve.

"You could put your dog out," she suggested grumpily.

Peter grinned. "You're very sexy when you're cross," he informed her. "Maybe we could go back upstairs…."

"And you can clean up after him," added Jane, managing to hold on to her temper. "I have other things to do." She swept from the room and went to sort out beds.

A great tide of plastic figures stretched from Christopher's bed to his door. Jane winced as her stockinged foot made contact with an unyielding tractor wheel. Peter can help him tidy this up, she decided, as she tugged the cover over the bed and folded his pyjamas. She made her way to the bathroom, then wished she hadn't.

The cleaned sink was now pock marked with toothpaste, the toilet was unflushed and a forlorn pink towel was draped across a pot of trailing ivy. Water seeped from a sodden flannel and dripped lazily to a puddle under the bath. Jane squeezed it furiously and returned it to the towel rail. Her children's thoughtlessness felt personal today and she resented the menial routine of clearing away their messes.

In her own bedroom a muddle of haste was dumped on the dressing table. Jane sorted cufflinks and coins, separating them from a folded handkerchief, a lipstick and her phone. She was surprised to see a message had arrived and pressed the button to illuminate the text.

"Hope you survive the day. Happy easter. Matthew"

Still holding the small phone, Jane sat on the bed and reread the message. A message, to her. From Matthew. Not a work related, essential message, but a personal friendly gesture. Jane scrolled through her menu and depressed the 'save' button. She felt suddenly warm and excited and very happy. She supposed that Peter had included her number in his long list of contact details that he had passed to the builders.

She read the message again. "It was sent today" she thought, "Today, when he is with his family. He must have thought about me, even if it was just for a second."

She rose and put the phone in a drawer stuffed with loose coins and car keys. She moved to the mirror and smoothed her hair down over her ears, pausing when her hands met her neck. "Not too plain," she told her reflection. Sparkling eyes looked back at her and her mouth curved up at the corners.

She would not mention the text to Peter, she decided, feeling intuitively that he would overreact and disapprove of the friendship. "Not that there's anything wrong," she reassured herself. How could something that made her feel so completely happy be wrong?

She felt that Matthew's friendship, however temporary, was a gift, an unsought after reward. "It makes me a better person," she mused as she straightened pillows and hooked back curtains. "When I'm happy, I'm a better wife and mother. My cheerfulness improves life for the whole family.

"It's a totally positive thing," she asserted as she sorted a clean towel for the downstairs bathroom. "How could anything so innocent and beautiful be harmful in any way?"

#

The window sill in the hall was crowded with cards. Christopher's playgroup chick held pride of place in the centre, next to a more delicate offering from Abigail bearing tissue paper flowers. Daphne had sent a flamboyant affair of folded card and bows that toppled over whenever the front door was opened. She had promised to visit soon. Jane wasn't sure if her presence today would have made matters better or worse. The two mothers did not like each other, so probably worse; but a 'Grandma War' would detract attention from the meal.

There was also a tiny card from Sophia to Christopher. It had arrived with Saturday's post and he had been terribly excited to receive a 'real' letter. It had a glossy picture of a duckling and inside Trisha had printed, "To Christopher, Love Sophia." Sophia had carefully written over her name with a green pencil. Jane had been surprised by the gesture. Maybe she had judged Trisha unfairly and should invite Sophia to play. One day….

Abigail appeared at her side.

"You look happier," she remarked. "Did you remember to heat the oven?"

"Oh Damn!" exclaimed Jane, "I knew I'd forget! Oh well, I don't suppose it makes much difference, I'll just put the meat in now."

Abigail followed her to the kitchen and watched as she removed the turkey roll from the fridge and placed it on the roasting tin.

"I hope there'll be enough," she worried as she put it in the oven and set the temperature according to the information on the packet.

"I'll do it a bit hotter," she decided, "to make up for not preheating the oven."

She carried the heavy saucepan of potatoes to the stove, ready to boil them prior to roasting. The wet underside fizzed as it made contact with the hot hob. Jane added salt and replaced the lid. Abigail was inspecting her nails. Her father had persuaded her to remove the indigo varnish and six of her eight necklaces. Her hands looked strangely nude without polish and she wondered if red would be more acceptable.

The doorbell rang.

"They're early!" said Jane in despair, as she ushered Abigail to the front door.

"Peter!" she called, "Your parents are here!"

Her leg caught on the hall chair as she passed, sending a snag running up her tights. Too late to change them now.

Christopher appeared on the stairs, wearing red lipstick around his mouth and Abigail's shoes.

"You've been in my bedroom again," protested his sister as Jane swung open the front door. She smiled a welcome into the ice blue eyes of her mother-in-law as the dog began to bark at the overflowing saucepan on the stove.

Hilary swept into the house, stooping to touch cheeks with Jane as she passed. Jane caught a whiff of expensive perfume, and remembered her own, pine-fresh-toilet, scent.

She was followed by the slightly hunched George who attempted to hug Jane through carrier bags of chocolate eggs and a large bottle of wine. He smelt of mothballs, which seemed appropriate.

"Hello Mum," smiled Peter as he appeared in the hallway, and moved to kiss her. "Jane, why is Max barking? Mum, Dad, come into the lounge and I'll pour you a drink. Happy Easter."

Jane escaped with Christopher into the kitchen to scrub his face. Abigail chose to trail after her grandparents. Her grandfather's bag looked worthy of interest, plus she would rather listen to adults talk than help her mother.

109

Hilary marched into the lounge. Her sweeping gaze noticed the clock was slow, there was dust on the lamp-shade and someone had pushed a book under the sofa. She turned her attention to her eldest son.

Hilary was a handsome woman. She was very tall and carried herself straight-backed with head held high. Her hair, once blonde, had faded to a dignified grey, trimmed and curled regularly at an expensive salon. Her pastel jacket exactly matched the shade of her shoes and handbag. Never without pink lipstick and pearls, she considered trousers on a woman to be common and refused to own a pair. One did, after all, have standards.

She sat stiffly on the window seat, while Peter poured sherry into tall thin glasses. They were seldom used and the pedestals were dusty. Peter surreptitiously wiped them with a tissue before filling them with the rich red wine. His father hovered behind him.

"I'll go and see if Jane needs any help," he suggested. "Rather grim to be stuck in the kitchen when guests are here. Shall I take her a sherry?"

"No!" replied Peter sharply, "Not a good idea. Not a good idea at all." He knew his wife's alcohol tolerance, and a tipsy Jane and his mother would make an unhappy combination.

Surprised but compliant - he had had many years to learn compliance - George made his way to the kitchen. Jane, looking somewhat hassled, was reading the instructions on a packet of frozen sprouts. The vegetables lay in a sodden heap in a saucepan of cold water.

"Place in a pan of boiling water," Jane read. Did it matter? Surely water was water, and the cooking time would begin when the water reached boiling point, irrespective of when the sprouts were added. "How would they know anyway?" she muttered as she threw away the bag and turned on the heat below the saucepan. She looked up as George came in.

"Hello Jane, need any help?" he said, taking a seat at the table.

"No thanks, it's all under control," lied Jane, as she scrabbled in the depths of the freezer for a bag of carrots. Past the de-boxed pizza, down at the bottom, with the frozen plums.

"How are you and Hilary? Keeping well?" She used a knife to slit open the top of the bag then poured the carrots onto a plate.

"Can't complain, thank you," said George, "Though I've had a bit of trouble with my leg lately. I can barely walk some days. And the gout is bad at the moment. Feels like someone is sticking pins into the end of my toes. Awfully painful it is, very bad."

"Oh dear," said Jane, wishing he would go away, "can the doctor not give you anything?"

She looked at the carrots. They were very orange. Described on the packet as "*baby carrots*" they were a uniform shape, but vastly different sizes. Jane felt sure they should be a similar size in order for them all to cook evenly. She pulled a knife from the drawer.

"Doctors today know very little," stated George. "They take one look at you, then tell you that at your age these things are bound to happen. In this country today, it's only the young who can expect any decent care. Once you're over a certain age, everyone thinks a bit of discomfort and pain is normal. They ought to remember who paid for the national health service in the first place."

"Oh dear," said Jane, again. She was concentrating more on the carrots than the conversation. There was something not very real about them, they were too orange, too triangular. "Do you still play golf?"

She pressed the knife into the centre of a particularly large carrot. Nothing happened. There was not even a tiny dent. The swollen vegetable sat unharmed on the plate, condensation beginning to form on its icy surface.

"Can't play golf with a bad leg," pronounced George. "Anyway, the club has taken on a new groundsman and he doesn't keep the lawns in very good shape. If the grass is in poor condition then that affects the game. No real standards anymore Jane. People are very sloppy these days. There's no pride taken in a job well done. Everyone thinks that 'good enough' will do. Well it doesn't, not in my book. If you are going to do something, do it properly."

"Er, yes," agreed Jane absently as she pulled a serrated sharp knife from the block. "Do you see much of Donald?"

She began to saw at the carrot, backwards and forwards, trying to dent the surface. The knife lost tension with the surface of the iced carrot and slid sideways, cutting her finger. She didn't swear. A drop of blood seeped from her finger and ran towards the carrot. She glanced at George. He was stroking the dog's ears, sipping his sherry, not watching. She moved to the tap, rinsed her finger and the carrot, and wound kitchen-roll around the cut. It would stop bleeding in a second. There was a plaster in a drawer, so she found it, stuck it over the cut, all the time keeping her back to George, so he couldn't see. George was talking about Donald, the favourite son. He hadn't noticed her silence, or what she was doing.

She inched open the knife drawer, and found the biggest, sharpest knife she owned. The sort of knife you could kill a burglar with. She placed the knife blade on the carrot and applied pressure. Nothing happened.

She leaned more heavily, increasing the force on the knife. Nothing happened.

"Of course, Donald telephones every week," George was saying with pride. "I suppose being single, he feels a sense of duty towards us. He's doing very well at work I believe. Has made a very nice life for himself. Of course, it's easier for him, not being married. He doesn't have all the worry and stress of a family man, and he can spend his hard earned income how he wants to. He's done a lot of travelling this year. Took a cruise down the Nile - Oh I say!"

Jane had pushed down with all her might on the knife. In sudden protest, and with a loud bang, the carrot had split in two, one half skidding across the work surface towards the cooker, the other taking flight and landing on George's shoe.

Jane felt laughter bubble wildly inside her and quickly bent to retrieve the orange missile before Max reached it. George stood up.

"I think I will rejoin Hilary in the lounge," he said, as he strode from the kitchen. For one outrageously mad moment Jane considered throwing the carrot at his departing head, then sanity returned and she placed it in the bin. She glared at the carrots. They would have to be cooked as they were. She tipped them into a saucepan and covered them with water.

#

By the time dinner was served, Jane was exhausted. She carried the hot tureens into the dining room and asked Peter to call everyone for lunch. Christopher arrived looking faintly sick and rather brown. Jane guessed that the Easter eggs had been distributed in her absence and that no one had thought to control their consumption. Perhaps, she thought, one forgot about the gluttony of a young child when contact with them was so limited.

With a child seated either side of her, Jane beckoned to Hilary to serve herself. She watched as her mother-in-law lifted a turgid spoonful of mushy sprouts onto her plate. Peter was standing, carving the dried turkey roll and passing slices to waiting plates.

"These potatoes look lovely," said Peter, hoping others would follow his lead and offer some praise for her efforts.

"Mine is all black inside," commented Abigail as she tried to slice a rubbery carrot.

"Always best to cook pork well," said George.

"It's turkey," said Abigail.

Hilary could not speak, having bitten rather heavily on a crunchy lump of stuffing which she suspected may have broken a tooth. She took a large swallow of wine, then added more gravy to her meal, in the hope of softening it.

"The gravy," thought Jane, "is really rather nice. I heated that at least to perfection…"

After a small dinner - "George and I never eat much mid day," - followed by a slither of apple pie that tasted suspiciously of cardboard - "I wonder if I should have taken it out of the box before microwaving"; the family retired to the lounge.

Peter helped Jane to clear the table then carried a large tray of coffees into the lounge. He perched it precariously on the coffee table.

"Will you have a coffee Dad?"

"Lovely," said George.

"Oh no," said Hilary, "he shouldn't have caffeine. Perhaps a herbal tea?"

"I would rather like a coffee…" ventured George.

"We probably don't have herbal tea," began Peter.

"Then water," said Hilary. "Abigail, please go to the kitchen and bring Grandpa a glass of water."

Abigail happily fled, sensing the tension. Jane sat in silence. Her thoughts were in Bath, wondering if Matthew had finished his lunch. She could imagine his family laughing together as they shared news and opinions. She smiled absently as she sipped her bitter coffee.

"This is fun," she thought, "I have a whole secret inside of me that they know nothing about. I look the same, and I act the same, but inside I'm different now. Inside I'm free and nothing else matters anymore."

She was suddenly aware of a lull in the conversation and looked up to see everyone staring at her expectantly.

"Jane?" prompted Peter, "Mum asked if we had decided on a school yet for Chris."

"Oh, sorry," apologised Jane in confusion, "I must be tired. I was - I wasn't really listening. Sorry. I expect he'll attend the local village school. Abi was very happy there."

"I see," said Hilary, oozing disapproval. "Though one assumes your finances are somewhat more secure now. I wondered if perhaps you might have given the matter more thought. Especially as he is a boy. It does seem so much more worthwhile to pay to educate a man, don't you think?"

Jane wondered why Peter had left her to answer. Now it looked like the choice had been her decision, not a joint one. She frowned.

Peter rose, eager to divert the conversation to less provocative subjects.

"Have you seen the garden Mum? Poor old Jane spends hours keeping it nice and the builders have made a real mess of it."

"Yes, well," said Hilary, piqued at having been dissuaded from her mission. "One must keep proper control of one's employees. It doesn't pay to be weak." She didn't move from her chair. She had no desire to see the garden, it would be muddy.

Jane sat back and rested her head on the over-stuffed chair back.

"I don't care anymore," she thought, observing the exchanges and unperturbed by the barbs directed at her. "It doesn't matter how bossy or nasty Hilary is, or how vainly Peter tries to defend me. They all think I'm the same but I'm not. They matter less to me now. I have a life of my own and a part of me that they will never reach and try to manipulate."

She rose smoothly from the chair, smiling serenely. "Peter, why don't you show your parents your plans for your extension? I really ought to walk the dog.

As she glided from the room, she glanced down, and paused. That was odd. What had happened to the plaster she'd been wearing?

Chapter Thirteen

May sunshine streamed through the bedroom window, illuminating the pile of neatly folded laundry. Jane was pairing socks. A comforting task that busied her hands whilst allowing her mind to float free, lost in a conversation with Matthew. She was remembering his face as she had related an account of shopping with two children in tow, how one corner of his mouth turned up more than the other.

"I wonder where he lives," she thought. She had a vague knowledge of the approximate area but not the specific address. It suddenly became important to know. Leaving the washing, she slipped downstairs and removed the telephone directories from the stack in the hall. She carried them quietly to the lounge and sat guiltily in a puddle of sunlight on the carpet. Her heart beat faster and a smile played on her mouth. Feeling like a naughty child, she searched for his name.

First she tried the directory of local tradesmen. She flicked through the pages of builders, recognising the names of people who had provided quotations for their project but no Matthew.

She heaved the larger directory onto her lap and turned the thin pages, chanting the alphabet as she sought his surname. E, F, G. Ga, Ge, Go. Her finger ran down the list of names then stopped. There it was. Half way down the list on the page labelled "private residential" was his name.

Reaching for a pen she copied the address onto the back of a flyer advertising cheap food at a new discount supermarket. She touched the words she had written, wondering what his home would be like. It was not in an area she had ever visited, though she had driven fairly near a few times when visiting one of Peter's aunts. Perhaps she could go there one evening, not to visit, but just to look. If it was evening, the lights might be on but the curtains open, she could watch him, see how he behaved in his own space when no one was there. She could stand outside, watch what he did. Though, it might be hard to explain what she was doing if someone noticed her. It might make her look a bit odd. She would have to be careful.

Humming, she returned the directories to their slot in the corner of the hall, on a shelf below the telephone. Then she carried the flyer into the kitchen. It occurred to her that it would be impossible to explain why the address was there, should anyone notice it. It was easily remembered and she walked to the kitchen bin, tearing through the picture of lemonade and biscuits.

Abigail wandered through the open door. "What's that?" she asked, seeing her mother tearing up brightly coloured paper.

"Just rubbish. It's from that new shop near the library. Advertising cheap biscuits and stuff."

Abigail watched as her mother thoroughly shredded the paper until it resembled confetti, then she opened her hands and the tiny scraps drifted into the bin.

"I guess she really did *not* want cheap biscuits," thought Abigail, then knelt to stroke the dog.

#

It was early summer when it happened and the day began much like any other. The building work was almost finished and Mr Bobb's appearances were becoming fewer each day. Jane guessed he had started his next job and was leaving Matthew to complete the Wood's house. Jane had settled into a comfortable routine that involved a minimum of housework, with frequent visits to the garden to chat. She found herself declining offers of coffee mornings or pleas for help at church and schools, using the rather lame excuse of "The house needs so much work at the moment."

She was still unsure of her standing with the builder and only felt able to disturb him when offering coffee or passing on some information. However, she was ever aware of his proximity and when not actually with him she was inventing witty comments or reliving past conversations. She found she could accomplish a whole plethora of tasks while allowing her mind to meander through previous dialogues, remembering tones and gestures and savouring each glance. She was living more and more inside her own head. If Peter noticed her preoccupation, he declined to comment, though Jane was aware of Abigail watching her sometimes as if trying to fathom her thoughts.

On the day it happened, it was mid-morning and Jane had just entered the kitchen, smiling, with arms full of the never ending laundry, when the telephone rang. It was Suzie. She was crying.

Jane listened, numb, as her friend related the harsh facts: Sophia had run into the road. She had been hit by a car. She had died before reaching hospital.

There was no way to soften the account and Jane could think of no response. She gradually realised that she was holding her breath.

"How's Tricia?" she said, realising she should respond in some way.

"No one seems to know. Jenny Shaw phoned me. They don't know when the funeral is or anything. Playgroup will send flowers. They want some money from everyone. Do you think we should phone her? It's only just happened, but you know how we all are -" she gave a soft laugh, awkward, forced. "When something happens whoever hears first starts telling everyone else. It's all soon common knowledge."

Jane nodded, even though Suzie couldn't see her. Broken legs, broken marriages, lost jobs - the news whizzed round, sometimes embellished along the way, but known by most people within a few hours. But nothing like this. This wasn't juicy gossip, this wasn't something to sigh over and tell each other how awful it was and perhaps the person should've seen it coming. This was bigger than the gossip chain.

She realised she hadn't answered her friend's question and tried to think. "No. I don't know. I expect she just wants to be left on her own. What would you say anyway?" She could hear Suzie crying again.

"It's just so awful," said Suzie between snotty gulps, "and I feel so guilty. I never liked her and now this has happened. It could've been any of us Jane, any of the children could do it. It only takes a second…"

"I know," agreed Jane. She wondered if she should invite Suzie to the house or arrange to meet her, but she felt irritated. She had not wanted this news and she did not want to be disturbed at home. It was her time with Matthew. "I need to go," she said, "I'll phone you. Let me know if you hear any more."

"Oh!" Her friend sounded surprised. "See you at pick up then…"

Jane disconnected the phone and tried to marshall her thoughts. She felt nothing. Nothing.

"I should feel sad," she thought, "or guilty that it's not me. But I don't. I don't feel anything. I just don't want the news to get in the way of my time with Matthew. He's not here for much longer. And really, it doesn't have anything to do with me."

She turned towards a sound in the new doorway. Matthew stood there, leaning an arm against the peach coloured plaster and watching her.

"It doesn't ring if you just look at it!" he joked.

Jane realised she was staring trance-like at the phone.

"No," she said, trying to smile. "I had some bad news…"

She stepped backwards, knocking the dog's bowl and water slopped onto the tiles. "A little girl at Christopher's playgroup," she continued. "One of his friends, she had an accident. Ran in

120

front of a car." And then, without warning, Jane *did* feel something.

Perhaps it was having to say the words, perhaps it was the image that rushed into her mind, or the memory of that warm weight leaning against her on the playgroup carpet. But the finality, the unexpectedness, the very bigness of it, suddenly hit her like a physical wave. "She's... she didn't....she's..." Jane stopped, feeling her lips quiver. Her mind could not force her mouth to say the words.

Matthew crossed the kitchen in one fluid movement. He took her elbow and guided her to a chair.

"Sit," he commanded. Jane resisted the urge to lean into him and sank obediently.

"You've had a shock," he said, "I'll make you a drink. Got any brandy?"

Jane shook her head. "I'm okay. Really I am. Just a bit shaken. I don't like brandy."

"Tea then," said Matthew. "My mother swears by it."

Jane watched him move easily around her kitchen. It pleased her that he was so familiar with the space, that he knew where to find mugs and tea, was comfortable using her sink, her kettle. He placed the tea in front of her and sat next to her at the table. She felt the warmth of his knee touching her own, and she did not move away. Neither did he - though she could not be sure that he had noticed.

He gazed questioningly at her. "Should I phone someone for you?"

"No," said Jane, not voicing that his was the only company she wanted. She liked him being so close, wanting him nearer but not daring to move. She could feel the tiny space between them, could almost feel the warmth from him reaching her. They sat in silence for a while then he rose.

"I'd better get on," he said, "Is there anything else I can do?"

"Yes," thought Jane, "Put your arms around me and hold me and comfort me."

"No," said Jane. "Thanks for the tea."

#

Jane left home earlier than necessary to collect Christopher. Something within her needed to check her own children, to reassure herself that they were safe. When she arrived she found somber-faced mothers huddled in small groups. Several were crying and they spoke in hushed tones. Hungry for information they quizzed each other for facts, most of which seemed to originate from one of Tricia's closer friends. The same sentences were repeated, modified, repeated again. A bee-hive of information.

Suzie waved Jane to where she stood with another mother. It seemed that Sophia had been leaving her home for playgroup when the accident happened. The car had been parked on the road and Sophia had decided to walk around to the passenger door rather than sit in the back. She had darted from the rear of the car just as a delivery lorry had rushed past.

"She didn't stand a chance," a woman was saying, "and there was nothing that Tricia could do. She was only distracted for a second. She didn't even know that Sophia wasn't getting into her seat in the back. She was probably being naughty for a joke, you know what they're like."

Jane was relieved when the playgroup door opened, signalling the children were free to leave. Mrs Brown stepped outside and beckoned to the waiting carers.

"Now, I expect you have all heard the terrible news," she began, her voice authoritative. "We were told ourselves just after registration, and we decided it would be best to carry on as normal.

We have not told the children because it's much better that they hear from you.

"I recommend that you tell them the truth as simply as you can. Try not to give them too many details at first, not unless they ask, but do be prepared for a lot of questions. And do not be surprised by their reactions." She glanced at some of the red-eyed mothers. "Children all react in their own way. They might not be as emotional as you would expect, especially initially. Sometimes these things take time to sink in. Let the children's responses guide you into how much to say. If they don't seem interested, then don't worry - they might want to know more another time."

She looked around, not sure if all the women would take her advice. She was concerned about her charges, didn't want them frightened by silly mothers who gave them every tiny detail. Nor did she want this avoided, so the children were left insecure, not knowing whether to believe their mummy who said Sophia had gone on holiday, or Jimmy who was giving lurid descriptions of a horrific death.

"Try to keep things simple," Mrs Brown repeated, "it's easy to frighten children with details that only adults need to know. If they don't ask, don't say. If they do ask, answer them honestly."

She turned and went back into the classroom. "Right children, your mummies are ready. Let me see who's sitting on the carpet ready to go. Put your coat on properly Samuel. Tommy, let me help with that shoelace. Hanky, Jemima!" Her voice faded as she moved towards the children. No one listening would have guessed how anxious she was, how keen to be relieved of her duties that morning so she could go home and have a good cry in private, away from watchful eyes.

The mothers edged forward, wanting to see their off-spring. Jane found she had an almost physical need to hold Christopher, to see for herself that he was unharmed. His face was subdued as he came towards her, sensing that something was wrong. Jane hugged him and he tried to wriggle away.

"You're squashing me," he protested, "and now you've got green on you."

Jane saw that a deep green smear from his painting had been transferred to her sleeve.

"Don't worry, it will wash off." She led him to the car, firmly holding his hand and strapped him into his seat.

"Can Tommy come to play?" he asked, adding, "Sophia didn't come today. I 'spect she's got mumps!"

#

Jane waited until after lunch to tell Christopher. She sat him on her lap and held him close, unsure of how to begin.

"Christopher love, there's something that Mummy has to tell you."

He twisted on her knee so he could look at her and gazed deep into her eyes, trusting her completely. There was a serious tone to her voice, and he wanted her to know he was listening. He liked when they had special chats.

"There was an accident this morning and Sophia was very hurt. She died darling….."

Jane felt tears welling and her voice faltered. She coughed, forcing herself to continue.This mustn't be about her. "Sophia is in heaven now with God."

Christopher frowned, trying to understand what his mother was telling him.

"Can we go and see her?" he asked.

"No Chris," Jane paused. "We can't see her anymore now. Not until we are in Heaven - When we're old," she added, as if saying it could ensure her own child stayed safe.

Christopher was still. He knew what dead meant, because he'd seen dead animals. But it did not seem possible that state could apply to Sophia. He also knew that people died when they were very old, and that they went to live in heaven. That also seemed irrelevant. Obviously this was something important because of the way he was being told, but he could not quite grasp the fact of what was being said. He decided to think about it later. It upset him that his mother was sad so he wound his arms around her neck, pressing his face against hers.

"I love you," he whispered into her cheek. "Can I get down now?"

Jane released him and he slithered to the floor. She leant back into the chair, fighting to control emotions that were now crowding in, threatening to overwhelm her. She watched her son as he stood. He was so perfect, such a mix of baby and boy. She could not bear to lose him.... She stood abruptly, determined not to cry and cause him to be upset on her behalf. She wanted his sorrow, if any ever came, to be for his lost friend, not merely a reflection of adult suffering which he did not understand.

"Come on," she suggested, wanting him to stay close; "let's make some cakes together before Abigail comes home."

They traipsed into the kitchen and Jane began accumulating bowls, spoons and recipe while Christopher pushed a chair to the sink. He stood on it while washing his hands, wrinkling his nose when the water soaked his sleeve cuffs. He pushed the chair back to the table and watched the growing heap of ingredients, poking each one with a finger as it arrived on the table. Butter, bags of flour and sugar and a tall carton of cocoa.

"What are we making?"

"Chocolate buns," mumbled Jane, as she flicked through the recipe books. She weighed butter into a bowl, then placed it into the microwave to soften while she spooned sugar onto the scales. After three spoonfuls, an angry sizzling alerted her to boiling liquid butter in the microwave, much of which had sprayed the interior. She lifted out the hot bowl, warning Christopher not to touch it. She would clean the microwave later. Probably.

Christopher was busy placing paper cases into the bun tin, several to each hollow, while humming tunelessly. He watched Jane tip sugar into the melted fat. She passed him a large wooden spoon and invited him to stir. His chair was too low, so he decided to kneel, but the hard pine hurt his knees. He tried standing on the chair, but was then too high. Jane was searching the fridge for eggs so he cautiously lowered his bottom onto the table. This felt comfortable if rather daring and he continued stirring the mixture.

Jane turned, eggs in hand. "Christopher! You shouldn't sit on the table."

"Ov-erwise I can't reach," he pleaded.

Jane let it pass. She cracked the eggs into a cup then found a teaspoon to retrieve fragments of broken shell.

"Mummy?"

"Mmmm?" Jane chased the shell around the cup. She managed to ensnare it with the spoon but it always slithered free before she could raise it to the rim of the cup.

"Can Sophia be un-deaded again?"

Jane stopped fishing and placed the spoon on the table. She looked at Christopher. He was still diligently stirring, so she emptied the egg (complete with shell particles) into his bowl.

"No Chris, when we die it lasts forever. Sophia lives in a different place now, with God."

The boy was stirring furiously, enjoying the slippery feel of the mixture in the bowl.

"Can we eat these today?" he asked.

"When they're cooked," answered Jane, somewhat bemused by the subject change. She spooned flour onto the scales then removed the rather greasy spoon from her son. "I'll have a turn now," she said, "you finish the cases."

Christopher returned to the box of muffin cases and continued to line the tin. It was more difficult now as they stuck to his fingers and he was glad when the task was complete.

"All done!" he declared, and pushed the tin along the table. The cases floated in the draft like snowy autumn leaves, and rested in a heap at one end. "Ooops," giggled the boy.

He watched his mother add flour to the bowl, stirring slowly to combine the ingredients. He noticed the large tub of cocoa and pushed his nose inside. He found he could fit both his nose and chin into the container. It smelt warm and chocolatey. He sniffed. The fine powder swept into his nostrils and he sneezed, spraying the table with droplets of moist cocoa.

"Christopher!" said Jane, going to get a cloth to wipe both the boy and the table. She added cocoa to her mixture then moved to the kettle.

"You can finish stirring while I take Matthew a coffee."

She carried the drink into the new extension. Matthew knelt at one end, fixing skirting board to the wall.

"Oh thanks." He gazed around the room. "Well, what do you think? Almost finished now."

Jane looked at the dusty floor, the plaster speckled window and the conch pink walls. She imagined the cleaning, the painting of coat after coat of paint and the work to revive her garden.

"It's nice," she said, "but it's been so long, I can't imagine it finished. It doesn't feel like part of the house, I will always think of it as a building site."

"You'll like it when it's finished and we've gone and left you in peace. Try to imagine it with carpet and curtains."

Jane turned to return to the kitchen. "Oh Chris!"

Like a small brown monkey, Christopher was perched on the table, legs swinging free. The bowl was in his lap and his fingers were in his mouth. Jane crossed the room and removed the bowl from his sticky hands.

"There's only enough mixture left for two cakes," she protested. "You'll be sick."

"He looks like he needs a shave," laughed Matthew, following her into the kitchen and observing the chocolatey rim that surrounded Christopher's mouth and coated his chin. "What are you making?"

"A mess, mainly," said Jane, rinsing the cloth in warm water.

"Chocolate buns," announced the boy, "but not for Sophia, because she's dead." He stopped uncertainly and frowned. "Do people eat in heaven?"

"Ah," said Matthew, "Your mum told me about your friend. Not sure I know much about heaven, but I expect people eat - but only nice food."

"No veg-e-tables!" said Christopher, wriggling as Jane scrubbed his face. He held out his hands to be wiped, wishing the cloth was less rough.

"Probably," agreed Matthew. He sat on the only clean chair and watched Jane as she spooned the remaining batter into two bun cases and carried them to the oven.

"What do you know about heaven?" said Christopher.

"Not much really, only that it's nice. And full of good people."

"Do you think the accident hurt Sophia?" The child was serious now, concern flooding his face as he considered this new thought. "Do you think she cried?"

Matthew's voice was very gentle, "Well Chris, we don't really know, but I shouldn't think so. I expect it happened very quickly and Sophia suddenly found herself in heaven. Her mummy will be sad, and you will miss her sometimes, but I think Sophia is alright. Who knows, maybe she's watching you bake cakes."

Christopher grinned, glad to be reassured. Jane lifted him from the table and began to clean it. She scooped the worst mess into the bin, then returned with a cleaner cloth to wipe the rest. She stretched down to wipe the chairs, and could feel Matthew watching her. She moved slowly, pretending to concentrate. His tone of voice caused her stomach to flutter and whilst his theology was probably flawed, she was impressed by his manner towards her child.

"I wish..." she began to think, then stopped herself. Some thoughts were too dangerous.

She carried the dirty utensils to the sink and ran hot water over them. Christopher was now telling Matthew about his morning, but she could feel the builder still watching her. She turned and met his gaze. He smiled, very slowly, then bent to talk to her son.

#

At three-thirty, Abigail trundled towards the car, surprised that her mother was on time. Her bag was laden with a history project and she carried it awkwardly, bumping against one hip. It was a sunny afternoon, though still cool, and long shadows fell across the windscreen, obscuring her mother's face. She reached the car and stepped across the muddy grass verge into the back seat.

"Hi," she said, "you've got brown stuff in your hair."

"We made cakes," said Christopher. "But mummy burnt them."

"Lovely," sighed Abigail. She caught her mother's eye in the mirror and smiled. "Never mind, it's nice of you to try."

"How was your day?" said Jane.

"Okay, got lots of homework though."

"We have some sad news," began Jane, pausing to negotiate a roundabout and narrowly missing an elderly lady pulling a shopping trolley. A group of teenagers saw her coming and walked purposefully into the road. She resisted the urge to accelerate and

129

slowed while they straggled across the street. She wondered if she would make it home before Matthew left for the day.

"There was a road accident," she continued, turning abruptly into the High Street. "One of Christopher's friends was killed."

Abigail's eyes widened. "Was Chris there? Did he see it? Is he okay?" She looked searchingly at her younger sibling, checking for signs of trauma.

"No, no," said Jayne, "it happened at her home. Chris is fine. Just sad," she added uncertainly, not entirely sure of her son's feelings."

"Oh, I am sorry"

Jane was surprised by her daughter's concern, and felt rather proud of her thoughtfulness. She sped through an orange light and turned down the hill towards home. Christopher leaned back in his chair and gave a large yawn, stretching his mouth as wide as he could. He was aware that he was receiving more attention than usual and felt decidedly content. He wondered if Abigail would like her cakes. He was troubled that the burnt edges were shiny, but perhaps Abigail wouldn't notice.

#

Matthew left later than usual that day. He appeared in the kitchen as Jane was defrosting pizza for tea.

"I'm off now. Just wanted to check you're okay before I go. I know you've had a rough day."

Jane basked in his sympathy, searching her mind for a reason to encourage him to stay but could find none.

"No, I'm fine," she admitted, "but thanks for asking. Do you want a cake?" She gestured towards the two cakes, sitting forlornly on the plate. Abigail had looked at them and announced she was not hungry.

Matthew paused. The cakes sat solidly together, icing dribbling over the paper cases. They had smeared the icing on them when they had cooled, but it had run into the dip in the centre and they now appeared varnished rather than iced. The edges were very black.

"Oh thanks. They look, well, I think Christopher enjoyed making them. Maybe we should leave them for him to eat."

He turned and faced Jane, his mood becoming serious. "You're a good mummy you know," he said softly, "sometimes I wonder if you deserve to be happier…."

Jane was motionless, willing him to continue.

The door burst open and Abigail stomped in.

"All the ink has run out," she stormed, "I've got tons of homework and no pen to write with. What do you suggest?"

Jane sighed. "Maybe we could add water to the bottle and shake it a bit."

Matthew grinned and turned to leave. "Bye," he mouthed.

Jane watched him leave. He walked to his car and climbed in with easy movements. The engine sounded, and he was gone. Soon he would leave for good. The thought disturbed her and she tried to push it away as she poured water into the nearly empty ink bottle.

When the extension was finished, in a few days time, she might never see him again. She screwed the lid on the bottle, and shook it, then passed it to Abigail. She watched her fill her pen with the diluted ink and test it on an envelope. The blue was very pale and barely legible.

"Matthew will be gone, moved on to the next thing, and I'll still be here. I wont have anything left," thought Jane. "I'll be invisible again. I'll just be the person who helps everyone else have a life."

"It's a bit faint," remarked Abigail, "You can hardly see it. But it works, so I guess I wont worry."

"Will anyone notice?" wondered Jane.

Chapter Fourteen

The day of the funeral was dry but dull. It seemed appropriate that there should be no sun, as if the grey sky reflected Jane's mood. Christopher was safely installed with a neighbour, and she drove alone to the large Anglican church near the school. She abandoned her car with a long line of others, which were parked in the narrow lane.

A gaggle of playgroup mothers hovered near the church entrance, wearing somber colours and careful lipstick. They huddled against the cold and the occasion, wanting to be together but studiously avoiding each other's eyes.

One mother had taken upon herself the role of host, and was speaking too loudly. She hugged Jane when she arrived and meaningfully asked how she was. Hardly knowing her, and therefore somewhat nonplussed, Jane muttered noncommittally and sidled over to Suzie.

"Shall we go in?" she whispered.

Suzie nodded. "The playgroup teachers are already inside," she said, "we were just waiting for you and Lynne."

The last mother could be seen hurrying towards the church in unfamiliar heels. Her white petticoat was slightly longer than the black skirt, making her appear oddly indecent. She smiled in embarrassed apology for arriving last.

"Ah Lynne," the loud mother enthused, "We were wondering if you were coming. How ARE you dear? Isn't this just awful? To think, it could be any one of us you know. One can't judge poor Tricia."

Suzie made a low growl and grimaced at Jane. "Lets go in," she said, and led the mismatched group through the arched doorway.

132

The interior of the church was cool. The religious familiarity of high roof, stained-glass windows and stone floor was oddly comforting. There was something solid about the building, it had seen it all before, even such as this.

The line of women processed up the aisle towards an empty pew, heels clicking on the ancient floor. The church was full. People sat, either staring rigidly ahead or with head bowed, in prayer or distress.

Their pew was near the back and they shuffled crab-like along its length, then sat slightly squashed, with shoulders almost touching. The loud mother, now subdued, was observing which people were not in attendance. Jane could feel Suzie bristling beside her and wondered if she would intervene. They both sat, silent and uncomfortable beneath the span of the high beamed ceiling.

Jane's knees brushed against a garishly embroidered kneeling pad, hung for convenience on a small metal hook. She wondered who had decided orange was a good colour for a dove. Red prayer books were stacked in pairs on the narrow shelf in front of her. She crossed her legs carefully, wishing her black skirt was longer and cautiously raised her eyes, not sure if she really wanted to see what lay at the front of the church.

At first glance it was filled only with flowers. White lilies and chrysanthemums, tight pink rose buds, fronds of delicate greenery. Wreaths, and complicated arrangements full of bows and ribbons. Then, with a heart stilling jerk, she realised the coffin also rested there. Tiny, white, almost doll like in its petiteness.

"It's Christopher sized," she thought and her eyes pooled with unbidden tears. "Don't look," she told herself. "Don't look. Don't think."

The service was short and Jane heard very little. She watched Tricia's back for a while, sagging towards the man Jane assumed was her husband. A lady in a hat kept careful vigil and constantly passed her tissues. How was this bearable? Each time that Jane felt the emotion rising, started to imagine how it would feel to lose a child, she rammed those feelings back inside, down somewhere deep.

"Don't look. Don't think."

The vicar swooshed around in his pristine gown, speaking in deep tones about things that Jane shut her ears to. God felt so far away from that female jammed pew, and she did not want to let him in. She was in a dark place, and she wanted to wallow there alone. Anything else was too dangerous.

"Don't look. Don't think. Don't listen.

The congregation rose awkwardly to sing childhood hymns, the familiar tune blasting brightly from the organ. Only the vicar could muster any volume, most of the congregation following the words mutely. Jane stared rigidly at her hymnal throughout, not trusting her voice.

The age-old scent of the church mingled with the heavy perfume of lilies and she felt faintly sick. She concentrated hard on her queasiness, forcing physical worries to overcome emotional ones.

"Don't look. Don't think. Don't throw up."

People sat, easing carefully back onto the hard wooden seats. The vicar began to talk about Sophia and the child's face, happy, alive, flooded Jane's brain. The warmth of her little body, her bright eyes, the way she ran, still chubby where she was only just growing from a baby's body, her enthusiasm.

"Don't think. Don't look. Don't listen."

People bowed with shoulders hunched as the vicar prayed. There were murmurings and stifled sniffs as people fought to control their grief. There was no abandon here, no distraught wailing or heart rending sobs. The great body of the church was still, quiet, subdued; dignified even in the face of such tragedy.

"I wonder what everyone's thinking," thought Jane, "the ones who don't believe in God. What are they thinking when they bow their heads?"

She said an automated "Amen" and relaxed her shoulders. She could not pray, not here, not yet. To pray would be to open her mind and emotions, to be starkly honest. She felt too fragile. Even to pray for Tricia would be too dangerous, opening herself to too much light. Safer to huddle inside herself for a while longer, to hide until she could cope.

"Don't look. Don't think."

The service ended. The people rose and two young men walked forwards to claim the coffin. Red rimmed eyes showed they had an attachment to the child, and Jane wondered if they were uncles. They were very young, not much more than teenagers. Too young for such a heavy burden.

They lifted their weightless load with care and walked, one careful step after another, to the church door.

"Don't look. Don't think."

Gradually gaunt faced family followed them; a stream of bewilderment clad in black. There was a pause, almost a holding of breath, as though the congregation was testing the reality of the afternoon, trying to find a way to assimilate what had been experienced. Then slowly, as though given a cue, people began to move, to shuffle from their places and to filter out of the church, returning to their lives.

The women followed.

"Lovely service!" Jane heard, "I did think Tricia did well, don't you? And such a good number here. Though I am surprised Emma Smith didn't make it, I wonder if....."

Jane turned away, following the other women. They all wanted to leave, fleeing to the safety of their private lives. A few wanted to talk, to verbalise what they had experienced, but most wanted simply to escape. Jane felt like she'd been through a mangle.

Suzie touched her arm, "You okay?"

Tears welled, mirroring those of her friend's. She paused. "How is this bearable?" she began, then stopped. She took a breath, and nodded. "I'll call you."

She walked down the uneven path, her hand searching her pocket for car keys, intent on leaving, trying to make her thoughts follow some kind of order again.

Towards the back of the graveyard, huddled near the wall, she could see the forlorn group of mourners. Their grief was freer now - more tears, more arms flung in support around trembling shoulders.

"How can anyone bear this?" she repeated to herself. "How can you survive losing a child?" She averted her gaze and hurried to the sanctuary of her car.

"Don't look. Don't think."

For a moment she simply sat, trying to calm her emotions. Then she glanced at the time. Three o'clock. Matthew would still be working. The desire to see him was almost overwhelming. Still close to tears, she turned the key and started the engine.

She drove home blindly. No one honked her or screeched to a halt, so she assumed she must have stopped at junctions and driven safely, but she was aware of nothing until she turned into her road. Several cars were parked nearby but not Matthew's.

She slowed to a halt outside her house. The building work was nearly complete and the new room sat smugly against the existing house. From outside it looked too clean, but finished. Inside, pipes were laid, wires in place and plaster smoothed across the bricks. Matthew came less often now but he had been there when she left, and he had planned to work all day. All day. That meant at least four o'clock. Not before three o'clock.

An irrational rage surged through her. She had wanted to see him. She had *needed* to see him. He would have been kind, sympathetic, supportive. She had been on the brink of tears. Maybe she would have cried as she told him about her horrible afternoon. Perhaps he would have comforted her. Put an arm around her, held her close. How dare he just leave? He had said "all day," did she not have the right to expect him there? Could she rely on no one?

She flung herself from the car and slammed shut the door. Then she realised her house key was in the glove box so she had to clamber back inside. She banged her head against the rear view mirror and cried out with pain and frustration.

She banged shut the glove box and it fell open again in protest. She glowered at it darkly. Leaving it hanging open she heaved herself out of the car and glared up the road, reciting swear words in her head.

Her neighbour's door opened and a concerned face appeared.

She thought about saying the swear words aloud.

"Oh Jane, I heard a car, and wondered if it was you. Did it go alright? I'll call Christopher for you, he's been ever so good."

Jane showed her teeth in an effort to smile and forced herself to breathe. Her anger dissipated as quickly as it had appeared, leaving her drained of energy and close to tears. Christopher arrived, pink faced from watching too much television. He put his hand in hers, confident she was pleased to see him. She thanked her neighbour, and took him home.

#

It was not until later that day, as they were driving Abigail home from school, that Christopher mentioned the funeral.

"Did you see Sophia go to heaven?" he said.

Jane glanced at him in her rear view mirror. He seemed relaxed, just interested.

"Well, not really -" she began.

"You don't see people going to heaven," Abigail interrupted, "You put them in a coffin and bury them."

"Under the ground?"

"Yes."

Jane saw fear begin to cloud his eyes. "Abigail," she said, "It's not like that at all. Sophia is in heaven, Chris, but she didn't need her body anymore so her mummy put it in a special box to keep it safe."

There was a pause as he considered this. "Where?" he asked.

"In the churchyard," said Jane quietly.

"Can I see?"

Jane didn't know. "Be open and honest" had been the advice, but how open? She knew that the children had been close friends, unusually so for their age. Plus, Christopher was a thoughtful child who liked direct answers to his questions and worried if he thought he was being evaded.

She decided she would take him. Today, now. He could see the grave while the flowers were still fresh, he would like that.

"Get it over with," she decided, "help him to understand."

She turned the car towards the church, driving in silence until they were parked. She twisted in her seat and faced Abigail.

"Do you want to wait in the car or come too?" she asked.

"I'll come," said Abigail, "I want to see too."

They walked past crumbling gravestones, along the moss patched pathways towards the section reserved for more recent deaths next to the wall. Jane held Christopher's hand lest he should run across the grassy mounds. Abigail followed.

The sun was beginning to shine, and afternoon shadows reached across the graveyard. A bird fluttered from the old stone wall, indignant at the disturbance, and a warm breeze moved the leaves on the ancient chestnut tree. Somewhere a wood-pigeon hooted.

Jane had been concerned that mourners may still linger at the graveside, but they were alone, free to approach the fresh heap of soil strewn with flowers. There were fresh graves on either side, slightly older, but still littered with bouquets and messages. The mounds of earth were bigger than Sophia's grave, but the flowers were fewer. A small wooden cross named the plot and they stood close together, smelling the earth and watching a bee as it collected pollen from the bouquets.

"Can she still come and play?"

"No Chris, I told you, she's in heaven now."

"In the clouds?"

"Yes."

"With God?"

"Yes."

"Did she take her bike?"

"No. Maybe God has bikes though."

"Oh." He thought carefully. "Can she catch all the balloons that blow away?"

"I don't know Chris, maybe.."

"Come on Chris," said Abigail, suddenly restless. "She's in heaven, and she'll be fine. Let's just go home."

She turned and walked away. Jane began to follow when Christopher jerked his hand away from her.

"Wait," he said. "I need to do something." Jane watched. He marched straight to another grave, his short legs determined, a frown on his face. Then he knelt, his sturdy arms reached for a yellow rose, which he tugged free from a wreath, crushing bows and flowers as he did so. He marched back to Sophia's grave and stopped. He again knelt, and very gently laid his prize next to a display of lilies.

As he knelt on the damp soil, his chubby fingers splayed on the mud, he peered intently downwards.

"Bye, bye, Sophia," he whispered. "Save a place for me."

Abigail began to giggle - halting abruptly as she turned to her mother's face.

Jane was completely still, warm fat tears falling to her chin and dripping onto her scarf. Something inside was breaking, and she didn't know how to stop it.

Abigail took her brother's grubby hand and led the way silently back to the car.

#

Peter arrived home late. Jane was yet again wiping surfaces, trying to remove still more plaster dust. It seemed to settle everywhere, a constant stream emerging magically in the air. Even now, weeks after they had applied the plaster, a fine veil of white had settled on the window ledge.

She heard Peter's key in the lock, the slam of the door and the bump of his briefcase landing in the corner. She poured herself a glass of water as he hung his coat in the cupboard, before pushing open the kitchen door. Side stepping the cat, he moved to kiss her head.

"Ugh, what a day," he groaned, pulling cheese from the fridge and reaching for a knife.

Max's tail began a rhythmic thump on the floor and he scratched the dog's ears absently. "I had back to back meetings all morning, and spent the afternoon playing catch up. Then the trains were up the creek due to a jumper at Waterloo. Honestly Jane, you don't know how much I envy you, here at home all day."

He trimmed a slice of cheese, perfectly even, and laid it across his bread. Jane wished he would use a plate. She offered him coffee and rose to fill the kettle. He noticed her face.

"You okay?"

"It was the funeral today, Christopher's friend."

"Oh yes," he said, remembering. He frowned. "You didn't take him did you? Bit tough on a child, don't think that was a good idea...."

"No, no," said Jane quickly. "I went on my own. I did take him to the grave afterwards. He asked to go. I thought it might help him," she finished defensively.

"Can't say I agree," Peter muttered, cutting another slice of cheese and admiring how perfectly symmetrical it was. "Best forgotten I'd have thought. He's only little, you could say she's moved away or something if he asked." His tone was disapproving.

Jane dumped his drink on the table in front of him, splashing some over the edge. It formed a milky rim, sealing the cup loosely to the table. Peter sighed and reached for the roll of paper towel.

"After all," he said to her departing back, "It's not as if she's a relative or anything."

Chapter Fifteen

The following morning, there was a note. Jane found it when she blundered into the kitchen to make tea. She had been asleep when Peter went to bed the previous evening and he had left early that morning, rushing to meet a client.

It was written on lined paper, torn from the pad used by Abigail for her homework. He had folded it in half and written sideways across the lines. It gave the words the appearance of having been enclosed behind prison bars. Jane found it propped up against the kettle, jammed upright by the pepper pot.

Darling,

Sorry about last night, realise I wasn't too caring. Phoned Izzy and she said you did exactly the right thing with Chris and that I was a self-absorbed brute.

Forgive me?

Oceans of love,

Pete xxx

She read it standing by the window. She wondered idly why he'd needed to phone his work colleague so late in the evening. Then she scrumpled it lightly and smiled. Matthew's car had pulled up outside.

#

Jane watched the completion of the extension with a growing sense of resignation. Peter, spending whole weekends locked inside with a paint roller or dragging her reluctantly round carpet shops, was perplexed by her lack of enthusiasm. He had assumed that the final departure of Mr Bobb would be heralded with delight and that Jane's rather discontented demeanour would return to the complaisant wife of previous months. But he was wrong.

Jane spent long hours doing nothing. She told herself that she was playing with Christopher but instead she would sit listless, remembering past conversations. She missed Matthew with an almost physical ache. His interest in her had caused her to come alive - her, Jane the person, not just the wife or the mother. Now she felt she was dying.

When she drove the children to school she was ever watchful for his car. When she returned home she would sometimes sit unseeing before the television, the film in her head creating tender moments that would never happen. She imagined his arms around her, strong and protective. His hand stroking her hair, smoothing her skin. His eyes, always intense, searching her soul as he kissed her. She created places they would visit, days when they would wander hand in hand sharing thoughts and jokes. Scenes of passion when all control would evaporate. Gradually, these thoughts and dreams became part of her life, reality an unwelcome interruption.

She grew irritable when the children demanded her attention, resenting their intrusion into her imaginary world. She stopped answering the telephone and ignored invitations to social events. Peter became an inconvenience, the creator of actions that must be followed automatically, an irritation to be pacified.

It proved to be surprisingly easy to avoid people. Jane realised for the first time how lonely her life was. Whilst she did not wish for the return of Mr Bobb, his intrusion had made a large impact, now there was an empty space. No one noticed when she returned home. No one knew what she did when she was there.

As her listless approach to life grew, so did Peter's concern. He had grown used to a wife who, though not efficient, had always tried. He could read despondency in her careless appearance, her long sighs, her constant frown. He felt he should act. He phoned Daphne.

#

Daphne arrived on a Wednesday. She had left her florist shop in the disgruntled hands of the woman she employed as manager, with Rachel to help. Rachel was sixteen and by her own admission 'not academic.' She had left school at the first opportunity and charmed Daphne into paying her very little for regular employment. She was now busy charming customers, which went some way towards balancing her total ignorance of plants and rather numerous piercings

The shop represented independence and self-esteem. When she found herself a single parent, Daphne quickly realised what little help she would receive after the initial offers and advice following the funeral. Everyone returned to their own lives, and she was left to raise Jane as best she could. She had always felt herself to be rootless and desired stability above all else. So she had found someone to sit with Jane in the evenings and had taken herself to night school. Her natural flair for shape and colour had made flower arranging a joy and she soon received private commissions to supplement her hours in the local shop. When the lease became vacant she had saved enough to buy out the retiring owner and her business was launched.

Now, as the train carried her towards her daughter, Daphne began to contemplate Peter's call. He had said that he thought Jane was depressed. She knew she had been shaken by the death of a child but that had been several weeks ago. Jane had always been a dreamer but Daphne was surprised to hear her described as depressed. She felt her daughter had rather drifted through life. As a child she was always reading or singing, living in a fantasy world surrounded by lots of pastel pink. She was an easy child, with few opinions, always happy to comply with other's wishes. Even later, as a young adult, Daphne was never sure if she had decided on jobs, homes, husband or simply drifted into them; moving contentedly through open doors without considering what might be behind others. As a working mother, Daphne had rejoiced in this compliance, grateful to avoid teenage rebellions or battles of will.

When Jane had married Peter, Daphne was content. Undoubtedly he was not the most exciting man that she could have married, but he was pleasant enough and seemed to care for her. Above all, he could offer Jane security and this, Daphne knew, was worth far more than all the charisma in the world.

She planned to stay with Jane for two days. She could help with the children and talk to her daughter, find out what was wrong. Daphne suspected she was just tired, worn out by the disruption of builders.

The train slowed as it neared the station. She raised the handle of her pull-along case and glanced along the carriage, selecting a man to help her. She saw one who was heaving his own bag from the overhead rack, nearly concussing the man below. Daphne held a variety of carrier bags above her own case, and hovered near to the doors he would exit from. As they hissed open she turned to catch his eye and smiled.

"Let me help you with that," he offered, lifting her bag down onto the platform.

She smiled her thanks and stepped from the train, searching for her daughter's face.

Jane hugged her mother, lifted her case and led the way to the station car park. Her car was marooned near the exit, blocking the flow of traffic in both directions. A dark blue Mercedes was behind, the driver glaring at her over the steering wheel. A yellow van was also attempting to enter the car park, the driver deciding that using his horn would speed things up. He began to press on it, the loud honks causing everyone else to turn and stare.

"Oh dear," wailed Jane, flustered. "I was late and there were no spaces. I didn't think anyone would come."

"Don't worry," smiled Daphne, "I like to make an entrance." She waved a purple and orange scarf at the Mercedes and winked at the van driver as she climbed into Jane's car.

Jane giggled.

"You are outrageous," she said as the engine fired then stalled. "Hell! This is not going well." The motor started and Jane edged red-faced around the van, the Mercedes glued to her tail. He followed her out the exit, and stayed dangerously close until the next junction when thankfully, with great roaring of engine he sped in the opposite direction. Jane sank into the her seat and looked at her mother.

"Welcome to my life."

#

Jane had put a temporary bed in the new room. Daphne approved the blue carpet, the patterned curtains and the oak desk laden with an uninstalled computer box. The room smelt of new carpet and fresh paint and the sun streamed through the window. It was a nice space. Daphne would have added a rug, some corner shelves, a plant or two and a large wood framed picture. These suggestions could wait though, she sensed her daughter was not feeling creative.

"I'll make some tea," said Jane, "then I must clean the sinks. They're getting very unhygienic."

Daphne was not sure if she was being avoided but decided to comply and took a magazine into the lounge. She moved a plastic policeman, a sock and some discarded homework notes so that there was space to sit on the sofa. A mug half full of cold coffee was balanced on a heap of newspapers, the milk congealed across the surface. A dried out plant sat wilting on the window sill. Unsorted clothes were dumped on a chair like an unstable slag heap; a cascade of underwear tangled with school shirts, a large red train engine balanced on top.

146

"Ooh, lovely," she said as Jane handed her a mug. "Let me know if I can help."

"No, you sit there," murmured Jane as she went in search of cloths and cleaning fluid. "I'm just fine."

She plodded upstairs to the bathroom. Plastic toys littered the bath, slimy from last night's bubbles. Stacking ducks lay with squirting toys, now filled with cold liquid. A large blue water wheel clung to the side of the bath, its suckers dyed pink over the years, its matching bucket gathering fluff under a bed somewhere.

Jane scooped out the toys and balanced them on the corner of the bath. She squirted yellow detergent onto the white enamel and wiped vigorously with a green cloth. Then she tackled the sink. Toothpaste encrusted taps leant over the grimy basin. Sighing, she looked up into the mirror. It was speckled with tiny droplets and her reflection stared back at her. Lank hair framed her face and she tried to recall if she had brushed it that morning. Her eyes were tired, purple shadows like bruises beneath them.

"I look old," she decided. "I feel old."

She began to wipe the scum off the porcelain. Abigail's toothbrush lay to one side and Jane saw that she had put it into a sandwich bag, obviously disdainful of the dirty sink. It had been enclosed while wet and the inside of the bag was damp. Jane removed it, placing it in the now clean mug to dry.

"Typical," she thought, "like her father. Expects perfection but won't help."

She knew that Peter had called her mother, and it irritated her. "*Mr Fixit,*" she labelled him. "Thinks every problem can be solved. But I can't be fixed and I'm his biggest problem to date."

She surveyed her work. The sink and tub gleamed, emitting a smell of bleach and lemon. Damp towels were still scattered across the floor and a pot of bubble bath sat in a green puddle.

147

Downstairs, something smashed. Jane left the bathroom and went to investigate.

#

In the kitchen, the cat was innocently washing her paws on the table. Max had hidden, face first, under a chair, tail hidden, ears flat. Daphne stood suspended in the doorway. The remains of a vase lay in lethal splinters across the floor.

Jane opened her mouth to speak. The telephone rang. Then someone banged on the door. The clock showed it was time to collect Christopher.

"You answer the door," sighed Jane. "I'll sort this. Let the phone go to answer machine." She opened the door to the garden, and Max escaped in relief. She practically threw the cat out after him. She began to sweep shards of glass into the dustpan. Daphne returned with an oversized envelope for Peter, and the vacuum cleaner.

"Shall I do this while you collect Chris?" she said.

Jane felt frazzled. "No!" she snapped. Then more gently added, "No, thanks, I've got time. Just....."

"Oh! but I need to collect some dry cleaning on the way home. Could you get the receipt for me? It's in Peter's wallet, which is in his brown jacket pocket - which I think is on the chair next to our bed.

"Thanks Mum," she called after her mother's departing back. She knew she was being churlish and that her mother was on her side really. With a sigh she returned to the broken vase.

Daphne climbed the stairs. Dog hairs matted the bottom few steps, becoming more sparse the higher she went. The carpet at the top was relatively clean. She pushed open the door to Jane's bedroom and waked to the side of the bed. She felt like an intruder in this room, feeling there was a special privacy to a couple's bedroom that should be respected, even by a mother.

She knelt on the carpet, next to a small tea stain and lifted Peter's jacket. The wallet was where Jane had guessed and she pulled it free. The soft brown leather bulged with notes and receipts and it unfolded in her hand. The pink receipt was easy to spot, its thick paper printed with days and a large tick scrawled next to WED. She was about to replace the wallet when the smiling eyes of a two year old Abigail beamed up at her.

Smiling, Daphne pulled free the small collection of photographs. Their corners were ragged and the shiny surfaces bent where they had been carried for years in the warm wallet. There was one of Jane, laughing on a beach in rolled up jeans and a shirt tied above her waist. Her legs were sandy and her hair bedraggled but Daphne knew it had been selected for her face which radiated happiness and love.

Next was a rather creased photograph of Christopher as a baby in his striped bouncy chair. The floor around him was a mass of toy animals and beside him Abigail clutched a sandy lion, its mane soft against her cheek.

There was a picture of Peter's mother, proudly holding a new born Christopher.

Daphne came to the last photograph. Her heart stopped. She remembered to breathe. Dry mouthed she attempted to swallow. The photograph was fairly recent and curled only slightly, with corners intact. It showed a young woman, handsome, with thick blonde hair that fell to her shoulders. She was smiling and behind her was the New York skyline. She was holding a raised glass of red wine, as though mocking Daphne for prying.

Hastily returning the pictures in their original order to their place in the wallet, she rose unsteadily to her feet. She looked down. The jacket and wallet were left as she had found them, but they now looked sinister, as if daring her to disclose their secret.

"Poor Jane, no wonder she's depressed," thought Daphne as she left the room, shivering slightly on the dark landing. "I wonder if she knows." Then she straightened her back and breathed deeply, reaching for the bannister with her free hand. "But it might not be what it seems," she reasoned with disbelief, "maybe that woman is a cousin. Or perhaps he put that picture in his wallet by mistake. Perhaps Jane knows all about that woman."

She heard the vacuum cleaner stop, its motor dying slowly, then the click as the plug was removed. She arrived in the kitchen to see Jane winding the grey cord around the handle.

"He must still love her, or he wouldn't have phoned me," her thoughts argued. "I'm sure we can sort this out. Jane mustn't do anything rash. She must not risk losing everything."

She smiled at her daughter and waved the pink ticket. "She mustn't let him escape. She needs her security…" She passed the ticket to Jane.

"Shall we go? It's getting late."

Daphne seemed preoccupied as they drove to playgroup and Jane welcomed the silence. She looked for Matthew's car as they came to the crossroads, searching the procession of cars as she waited at a red light. She slowed the car when passing a scaffolding-clad house, wondering who the contractors were. They arrived at playgroup.

"Shall I collect him?" offered Daphne, jumping from the car.

Jane nestled back in her seat, warmed by the sunshine. She remembered when she had hurt her finger and Matthew had held her hand. She breathed deeply, almost smelling him again. She disappeared within herself and dreamed.

Daphne joined the mothers waiting by the door. She recognised a thin, fair haired woman as Jane's friend and stood near her.

"Hello," said Suzie, "You're Jane's mum aren't you?"

Daphne smiled and nodded. Suzie opened her mouth as if to speak. She wanted to ask if she had offended Jane somehow, causing her to avoid her. Unsure of how to phrase it she simply smiled. The door opened, heralding the end of school for another day.

Daphne shuffled forwards until it was her turn at the head of the queue.

"Nana Nana!" exclaimed Christopher, waving a picture at her and straining forwards to be released.

The playgroup teacher kept a restraining hand on his shoulder. She had met Daphne on previous occasions but she feigned ignorance, choosing to make a point. She was tired, it had been a long morning; and these mothers were too casual, they took too much for granted.

"Oh," she said, "Mrs Woods did not inform us someone else would be collecting Christopher today."

"I'm not really someone else, I'm his grandmother."

"Well, we do like to be informed," continued Mrs Brown, "we do have our child protection policy. We were expecting Mrs Woods."

Daphne felt defensive. "Mrs Woods is in the car over there," she pointed out. "Shall I fetch her?"

Annoyed at being so easily thwarted Mrs Brown let go of Christopher and he hurtled towards his grandmother. He shoved the crumpled paper into her hand.

"I made you a dove. It has wings."

"Perhaps you could ask Mrs Woods to inform us in future if she needs to change the arrangements. We all want what's best for the children, don't we?" Mrs Brown turned to her next charge. "Ah Tommy, can you see your mummy? Don't forget your bag of wet trousers.

"We had a little accident," she informed Suzie.

Summarily dismissed, Daphne led Christopher to his mother's car.

Chapter Sixteen

Jane left Christopher chatting happily to Daphne while she prepared his lunch, and drove by herself into town. They had hung the dove by its loop of elastic in the window, its concertina wings unfolded on each side and its rather crooked eyes surveyed all as it swung in the breeze. It looked more like a used tissue than a dove. A used tissue with a drunk expression.

Jane parked in the supermarket carpark, because it was easiest and no-one ever checked, and hurried to the bank. Peter had left two cheques for her to pay in, then she would collect his clean suit. It was cool for June and Jane pulled her cardigan shut, wishing she had worn a jacket.

There was a line of people extending out of the bank and down two brick steps. Automatic doors had been installed on the old building and these were opening and shutting continually as the sensors detected the waiting customers. No one was willing to leave a gap large enough to allow the doors to close. Instead they annoyingly clanked open, paused, hissed shut, over and over again. It was going to be a tedious wait.

Gradually the line shuffled forwards until at last Jane was inside. Everything in the bank seemed to be grey, from the rough carpet to the plastic shelf littered with complimentary pens. She noted that there was only one service window open and guessed that most of the staff were having lunch. Behind the glass partition sat a tall young man. He wore a white tee shirt and his name clip was upside down. His voice was loud and he spoke with a Canadian accent. It would seem that he was following a security check with the lady who was waiting. As everyone was listening, it was not especially secure - more of an 'insecurity' check.

"This is a very large amount of money you wish to deposit, so I shall have to ask you some questions."

"Do you?" said the woman. She looked very unhappy, and was very conscious of all the waiting customers listening. "This is my own branch, is it necessary?"

"Yes. I do not recognise you and this is standard procedure. Now, what is your address?"

She recited an address that Jane recognised as one of the more affluent roads in the town. Several other people looked up, obviously interested and not bothering to hide that they were listening.

"And do you own or rent the property?"

"I own it," she said, as though aghast at the mere suggestion of rental.

"And do you have a mortgage on this property?" he persisted.

"No," she said. People's interest grew.

"How long have you lived at this address?"

"Six years. And I have always used this bank so I am surprised this is necessary!" she snapped. She was irritated and uncomfortable.

He continued unperturbed. "Just bear with me. Now, do you own any other properties?"

"No! Do you own a shirt and tie?" she retorted. Several people tittered.

He raised his eyebrows, then continued. "Yes, I do. Now, what do you intend to do with this money?"

"Well," she said, "I *had* intended to deposit it in my account, but that is proving difficult!

"Nearly there," he said, "I have to ask due to money laundering laws. Are you planning to spend this money soon?"

"Do I *look* like I'm laundering money?" she asked, clearly affronted.

To Jane's amusement he paused and looked hard at the woman. She was about fifty with smooth black hair and a designer handbag.

"No," he affirmed, "but I have to ask."

"We are having building work done," she said, bristling. "I am moving money so that I can pay the builder."

"That's okay then, all legal, have a nice day," he chanted, without the flicker of a smile.

The woman snorted, snatched her receipt and swept to the exit.

Jane approached the desk. She passed the cheques and her cheque book under the glass.

"Please could I pay these in?"

He looked at what she had handed him.

"Are these cheques being paid into the account on the cheque book?" he asked. Jane nodded.

"We do have blank paying-in slips available at the branch. All branches do. We request that customers fill them out before approaching the counter."

"Oh!" said Jane, red faced.

He pointed to the grey shelf that ran the length of the wall behind the queue of people. Jane retrieved the cheques and squeezed through the queue to the shelf. She found the white slips and searched for a free pen that actually had some ink left in it. On completion she turned back. The number of people waiting had not lessened and Jane realised she could not force her way back to the front of the line. Nor could she bear to rejoin the back. Tucking her papers into her bag she left, passing through the over worked doors into the sunshine. She would come back later she decided.

After collecting the dry-cleaning, she began to drive home. Her mind began to replay the conversation in the bank and she wondered who the unfortunate woman had employed to do her renovations. Instead of turning towards her home, Jane detoured via the road that had been mentioned.

It was a peaceful road. Bordered by a wide verge with tall hedges that hid the properties from enquiring eyes, the road ran along the outskirts of the town. It was little used other than by residents, though it did lead to a busier road. Jane drove slowly along its length, peering up each driveway as she passed. Towards the end, near a large oak tree, she was rewarded.

There, parked near to the road, was the red sports car. A skip had been parked further up the driveway. There was no other sign of work. No disturbed lawn, no scaffolding, no builders.

Jane turned back onto the main road heading home. A smile touched her mouth. She knew where he was. She had not seen him but his car was imprinted on her mind and she was certain it was his. Contented, she returned home.

#

The following day, Daphne took Jane out for lunch. A baby sitter had proved impossible at such short notice so Christopher was joining them. He was very excited and swung his legs in the back of the car until Jane told him to stop.

They had decided to eat in a pizza place in the town centre. It seemed relatively child friendly whilst still providing food that adults might enjoy. The restaurant had glass walls on two sides, so customers could watch shoppers hurrying past as they ate. It had a counter of fresh ingredients on a cooled surface waiting to be applied as pizza toppings. The floor was shiny, and the round tables each bore a single flower in a delicate vase. The chairs were fashionable and uncomfortable. The menus were super sized and Jane removed Christopher's before he sent the vase skidding across the table top.

They ordered quickly, the large glasses of red wine being more important than the food. Christopher was handed a picture and a small packet of crayons. Jane removed a red and began to colour a flower while her son waxed a stalk green. She wasn't really sure why her mother had suggested the outing, especially with Christopher in tow, but she supposed it might not be too bad.

Daphne sipped her wine, watching her daughter. She seemed tired but not ill, tense perhaps, but not especially depressed.

She planned to say very little, rather to provide opportunities for Jane to confide if she wanted to. It was a shame that Christopher was present but he was young enough to not understand too much. It would at least mean Jane couldn't avoid her, there had not been many opportunities to talk, and Daphne was unsure if this was by design. She was not used to her daughter avoiding her. If she knew of the affair (and the more Daphne thought about it, the more she was convinced there *was* an affair) then it was important that she should know her mother supported her. It was also important - possibly more so - that she did not do anything rash. It was always possible to move on from things, sometimes you just had to ride the storm.

"Peter's worried about you," she began.

"I'm fine," said Jane, shading in the branches of a tree.

"You are wonderful," corrected her mother. "But sometimes being a wife can be hard…"

"Like colouring is hard," added a frowning Christopher. "I keep going over the edges."

Jane concentrated on colouring a sun. Had her mother guessed her thoughts? Was she about to tell Jane to 'snap out of it', to get on with being a wife and a mother and to stop being moody? Had she sensed that Jane's mind was full of someone else?

Daphne continued, "Even when men love us, sometimes they can do silly things. They hurt us, sometimes very deeply. But it doesn't mean they don't love us."

Now Jane was confused.

"I'm not sure I understand what you're trying to say," she said.

"I got hurt," Christopher offered helpfully, "I fell off my chair and banged my elbow."

"I'm not saying anything dear," said Daphne looking worried. She took a large sip of wine. "I just want you to know I love you."

"So do I," said Christopher.

"And should you need support, I'm here for you. But," she added, "Don't make any hasty decisions. Don't decide things you might come to regret."

Christopher was not sure what 'regret' meant and remained silent, frowning at his picture.

Jane was saved from answering by the arrival of the food. She moved her wine and the child's beaker to the centre of the table and scooped the crayons back into the box. Christopher pulled his picture out of the way then released it, watching it float to the floor.

Jane used her cutlery to trim the pizza to bite sized pieces. The crust was tough and it proved a struggle with the blunt knife provided. A waiter with an over sized pepper mill offered seasoning, which Christopher accepted and Jane quickly refused on his behalf. He was picking up pizza pieces, checking the underside for burnt bits.

"Stop playing with your food," said Jane, cutting her pasta to let some heat escape.

Daphne tasted her food, then decided to try again. She might not find a better time, and there was no point in her coming if she couldn't give her daughter some advice.

"Sometimes," she said, fiddling with the stem of her glass and not meeting Jane's eyes, "sometimes, it seems like there is every reason to leave. But it's not necessarily the right thing in the long run. However bad things may seem, they usually settle down.

"Marriage is not always flowers and romance. Sometimes, life can seem impossibly tough…."

"This is tough," said Christopher, who had given up on the pizza base and was sucking the cheese topping off.

"You have to always plan for the future," Daphne continued. "Sometimes things can be really bad but they're still *good enough*. It is easy to overreact, to act impulsively and regret it later. Even if things are a bit wobbly for a while."

Christopher shuffled in his seat. Nope, it was very secure, nothing wobbly there at all.

"You might feel the need for change," said Daphne, "but you don't want to throw away all the good things too."

"No!" said Christopher, who was rather enjoying this adult conversation, "Like when you threw away my brown pyjamas. I liked them. You won't throw away my Winnie-the-Pooh ones, will you?"

Daphne looked her daughter in the eye.

"Think carefully," she advised, "about what you truly want."

Jane felt as though she was solving a riddle. 'What,' she wondered, 'is she trying to say?'

Christopher leaned forward, his nose almost touching Daphne's.

"What I truly want," he confided, "is to go to the toilet."

Daphne smiled and lifted him from the chair. Holding his hand she led him from the table, happy to abandon her conversation.

"Much better to just leave it," she decided, Jane would talk if she needed to.

She had never relished giving advice and preferred to keep her opinions private. But Jane was still her child. She wondered if you ever really stopped mothering, if there was ever a time when your work was finished.

Jane watched them walk hand in hand across the restaurant. Christopher was taking giant steps, throwing his whole little body forwards, his grandmother swinging her arm in time with him. They looked so complete, contented in their own world.

"I wonder," mused Jane, "I wonder if they ever have empty spaces inside of them." It seemed wholly unlikely. They turned the corner and she picked up her wine glass.

Glancing outside, she happened to see her mother-in-law, just as Hilary peeped through the glass. She was laden with groceries, which she lifted in greeting. Jane raised her glass in reply, then Hilary turned and was gone. Jane took a long slow swallow.

#

Jane took her mother back to the station on Friday afternoon, on her way to collect Abigail. Christopher had fallen asleep in his car seat, so she parked within view of the platform and helped Daphne with the case.

They stood together, not speaking, waiting. Jane kept glancing at the car, checking for signs of movement.

Daphne rummaged through her bag for her ticket. She felt mildly dissatisfied with her visit. The house was somewhat cleaner and she felt that Jane was not worryingly depressed. However, she was concerned for her daughter's marriage and was unsure of her role. How much should she interfere? The train drew into the station, doors hissing open, spewing out an old man and two rather guiltily faced school boys.

Daphne hugged Jane hard and kissed her cheek.

"Thanks Jane. Lovely to see you all," she said, then paused. "Do phone me whenever you want, wont you? I'm always there."

She stepped into the train, wanting to say more. "Maybe you and Peter should plan to go out one evening? Like a date? Have some fun," she suggested.

Jane waved as the doors shut, separating them. She was rather nonplussed by the random suggestion. Her and Peter never did things like that, they were too busy.

Daphne blew a kiss as the train slid away. Then she was gone.

Jane drove home lost in thought. Perhaps her mother's unexpected suggestion was a good one. Jane could barely remember the last time she and Peter had been out together on their own. Maybe it *was* time to try and remember why she had married him.

She pondered. Probably Mrs Lang at number four would babysit, they could be home before it was too late. They could have a meal, some wine. Chatting at home was different to talking in a restaurant. You behaved differently. It might be fun. They might manage to talk about something other than the children if they were slightly further away.

She drove into her driveway and turned the key.

Christopher woke and gazed with bleary eyes at the house. Then he looked across at the empty seat beside him. He looked at the back of Jane's head and frowned.

"Where's Abi?"

#

Jane sped angrily towards the school. How *could* she have forgotten her own child? She turned onto the main road behind a small white car that was determined to be at least ten miles below the speed limit. Jane could see a mound of grey curls above the driver's seat. There was a slight bend in the road, the car in front braked sharply. Jane hissed. She drove as near to its bumper as she dared as it crawled up the main road. The indicators flashed left. Then right. The car continued in a straight line.

"Come on, come on," moaned Jane as they slowed again when a lorry passed them in the opposite lane. She almost touched the bumper when it slowed almost to a stop. The windscreen wipers

161

careered across the dry glass and it turned left into a side road. Jane breathed deeply and zoomed to school. She realised her jaw was clenched.

The usually crowded street was empty and she easily found somewhere to park near the school gate. Abigail was leaning against the school fence, bag on floor, reading a book. She looked up as Jane opened the door and smiled.

"You're late!" she said, climbing into the back.

"I'm sorry. I had to take Nana to the station." Jane could not think of a good way to explain to her child that she had been forgotten.

Abigail leaned back in her seat and continued reading. Christopher tried to grab her book so she turned towards the window, using the novel to shade the streaming sunlight.

"Don't get car sick," warned Jane as she turned into the traffic. "How was school?"

"I *never* get car sick," said Abigail. "School was awful. It's always awful. Except for science. We went to a pond today. Tried to catch frogs but only saw water boatman."

She turned to Christopher. "They're little floaty insects," she explained, "and they have arms that look like oars. And they row across the water. On the skin," she added, trying to be accurate.

Christopher frowned, not liking the idea of insects on his skin. They might bite.

"Did you touch one?" he asked.

"No, we just shook them out the net into a jam jar. A specimen jar," she corrected. "Except for Simon Michaels. He dropped one on the floor and stamped on it. Mrs Jones told him off and took his net away.

"Oh, why are we going this way?"

They were travelling down a quiet side street, tree lined and exclusive. Jane was peering intently through the window.

"The traffic's bad on the main road," she said, "I thought we'd come this way."

There, third house from the end, was the red sports car. Jane continued to the end of the road. No sign of people, just his car. She sighed, then continued home.

Chapter Seventeen

Jane was under the kitchen table, cleaning up dog vomit, when Peter got home from work. Abigail had noticed it at tea time and protested loudly that it was "disgusting" and she could not eat any more dinner. She flounced from the room leaving untouched vegetables and the burnt end of a sausage on her plate.

Christopher chuckled and began to chant, "Dis-gusting, dis-gusting, dis-gusting...." Until Jane abandoned the table and hoisted him from his chair. He had then been bathed and bedded rather earlier than usual.

Now she was dealing with the mess, spatula and newspaper in hand. Peter bent down and peered at her.

"Hello, are you hiding? Oh, I see."

"Hello," she replied, her voice echoing under the table. Her knees hurt on the hard floor and this was not a job she relished.

"Please could you pass me the squirter?" she asked, flapping a hand towards the disinfectant.

"I've got my suit on," said Peter, distancing himself. "I'll help in a minute, when I've changed." He left, heading for the stairs.

"Can't see how his precious suit would get damaged just passing something," muttered Jane as she heaved herself up. "Seems to think he's God when he's wearing that blessed suit."

Images of Matthew, often messy, usually handling dirty substances, flooded her mind.

"Real men don't mind dirt," she thought.

#

The floor was clean when Peter returned. He was eating when Jane mentioned the idea of going out together one evening.

"Why?" he asked, "We see each other all the time, chat every day. Why spend the money?"

"It might be nice," said Jane. "We could go somewhere cheap. Just us."

"I expect Abigail would feel rather hurt not to be included," said Peter.

"Included in what?" asked his daughter, checking the floor before she entered the room.

"Your mother wants to go out for dinner one evening."

"Ooh yes," said Abigail, "can we?"

"No," said Peter. "Now go and finish your homework."

Jane followed her from the room. It was clearly a bad idea.

#

Jane was in the bath later, so did not hear the telephone ringing. The water was slightly too hot, stinging her skin as it lapped up to her neck. A pink ball of bath salts fizzed next to her, releasing the scent of roses. She closed her eyes, enjoying the solitude. An old sponge pillowed her head and her feet floated near the taps. Peace blanketed her.

Peter rapped on the door, making her jump. "Jane?"

"Yes?"

"That was Suzie on the phone," he shouted. "She wanted to speak to you. Said did you fancy going out for a drink. I said yes. Good timing! You'd just said that you wanted to go out somewhere. I arranged it for next Friday. Eight o'clock. I'll get home early and babysit for you. There! That should cheer you up."

He smiled as he walked downstairs. He loved his wife. It was good to do something she had asked. He felt very satisfied, pleased to have been a compliant husband.

"Your wish is my command," he said, as he collected a beer en route to the television.

#

"It may be a Friday evening," thought Jane, "but I do not want to go out."

165

She flung open the wardrobe door. Her reflection glared back at her from the mirror, hands on hips, mouth set in a straight line. Unable to face choosing clothes, she moved to her dressing table. A mound of washing, clean but unsorted sat at one end. It vied for position with a note from school, shop vouchers and a packet of shoe laces.

Pushing them to one side Jane reached for the mirror. Make-up. Eye shadow seemed too dressy, but she ran eye liner across her upper lids. It felt a long time since she had worn make-up. Had wanted to wear make-up.

"I still look tired," she decided as she tipped her lashes with black. "Too pale." She dusted pink on her cheeks and smoothed red lipstick over her mouth. She leaned back.

"Now I look like a clown. An old tired clown." Tears pricked her eyes and she sniffed them away, wiping off most of the red with a tissue. A trace of lipstick remained, echoing the pink of her nose and her red-rimmed eyes. She sighed. This was so much effort.

Pulling clean socks from her cupboard she struggled into black jeans. A roll of flesh bulging unattractively over the waistband was quickly covered by a soft pink sweater. She checked the mirror again.

"Not too bad." The pink was fading from her face, and her mood began to improve with her appearance. She scrabbled in the bottom of the wardrobe for black boots and buckled them tightly. "Getting there I think," she told herself. She snapped on tiny silver earrings, then fought with the catch of a necklace as the doorbell rang. Abandoning the necklace for a string of beads, she pulled a brush through her hair, then went in search of her coat.

Jane got into Suzie's car trying not to feel ungracious. She knew her friend was attempting to cheer her up. She was aware her

166

husband also thought he was being helpful. However, she still did not feel like going out and resented the intrusion.

Suzie suggested that they visit a pub that was just out of town. She chatted happily as she drove, seemingly oblivious to Jane's gloom. They left the town, houses giving way to fields and then trees. The roads narrowed to lanes and they meandered through a farm and into woodland. Jane sat still and silent, watching the countryside skim past.

"It's so pretty," she acknowledged, "but it doesn't reach me anymore. I feel like I am sinking into black treacle. I keep wading through it but it never washes off. Life has become such an effort."

Green light filtered through the branches that arched overhead, a tunnel leading onwards. Mud, packed hard, led in a thousand secret pathways into the woods, enticing walkers past gnarled trees that had stood for hundreds of years. A pond, fat and green, sat in a clearing, the black earth surrounding it sodden and glistening in the late evening sun. A dozen scenes, glimpsed in a second, as they drove past. As they turned a corner they saw a large yellow sign.

"This area is being monitored for litter," it declared in bold letters.

"Huh!" snorted Suzie, "Do you think that will make any difference? Maybe I should get one for my lounge!"

They turned into the car park, crunching slowly across the gravel and came to a rest next to a mud splattered Land Rover. Jane climbed out, noticing a bird's evening song as it carried on the warm air. She smiled and followed her friend.

Ducking through the low doorway they entered the fug of the pub. Men in wellingtons and cabled sweaters stood laughing in small groups, swigging from pint glasses and wiping their mouths and chins on the backs of their hands. They turned to appraise the women as they entered, then returned to their rumbling conversations.

167

Suzie wove her way to the bar and smiled as a tall bespectacled man came to serve her. She ordered wine and they carried their glasses to a tiny table in the corner. Jane pressed her back against the wall and surveyed the room as Suzie handed her a menu. The dark wood table was sticky to touch and she carefully put her glass on a curling mat.

Oak beams lowered the sagging ceiling, which looked as if it were ready to crumble. Worn brickwork surrounded a large fireplace, filled now with a pottery urn of grasses and dried flowers. A large photograph of Churchill dominated one wall, next to a faded copy of the Magna Carta. A high shelf carried beer mugs of all sizes, many cracked and all thinly coated with dust. Horse brasses hung from nails on the wooden pillars and a multicoloured carpet softened the floor. They could have been in almost any pub throughout the whole of England. Jane wondered how many people actually saw the decoration. Someone, at some time, had decided on a theme, collected everything, arranged it on the walls. Now it was unseen, part of the atmosphere but not really noticed.

Jane sipped her wine as she scanned the menu. It was printed on white card, encased between thick plastic that was smeared with grease, where someone had *almost* wiped off a buttery thumb print. Suzie was chatting, talking at speed, not really needing Jane to answer. She moved from playgroup stories, through scathing descriptions of other mothers, and onto exasperation with her husband. It occurred to Jane that the trip was maybe not exclusively for her own benefit. She smiled and nodded at all the right times, the words washing over her unheard.

The menu was short but comprehensive. Hot and cold starters were separated from main courses by a line of stars. Dinners ranged from pigeon pie through fish platters to the obligatory vegetarian dish tacked on the end. Jane thought they always sounded so unappetising, as though a meat loving chef had taken affront at so demeaning a request as to provide a vegetarian option. It invariably involved either nuts or lentils and conjured images of grey stodge with chewy lumps.

Jane chose fish pie. Not so much because she liked smoked haddock as because it would be easy to eat. She could effortlessly spoon hot food into her mouth with barely the need to chew. Suzie leant towards her, suddenly attentive.

"Do you see that mirror over there?" she said, her voice low. Jane followed her gaze and nodded.

"We get a view straight into the gents," said Suzy. As if on cue, the reflected door swung open and a man emerged, still zipping his trousers. Behind him was the back of a man who stood facing the wall.

Jane giggled, nearly spitting out wine.

"This could either be an excellent table or a very bad one," she said, then glanced at the group of sagging men at the bar. "I think a bad one."

Suzie went to place their food order at the bar, returning with more wine. Jane began to relax, the wine softening her mood as she looked around the bar.

Most of the men were beginning to drift away, returning home after their regular post-work drink. With them went the heavily masculine atmosphere that had pervaded the pub when they first arrived. There were no raised voices now as discussions grew less heated, no sudden bursts of laughter. One or two still lingered at the bar, leaning heavily and staring moodily into their beers whilst exchanging a few words with their fellow drinkers. They seemed to blend in with the dusty beer mugs, the faded flower arrangement.

Mostly they had been replaced by the evening clientele, couples coming for a quick drink or people arriving for dinner. The tables were all occupied and fewer people stood, just a group of young men who loitered near the door as though waiting for a friend.

The food arrived, with cutlery tightly wrapped in paper napkins. They ordered more wine and tasted the food. It was hot and rich and creamy. Jane felt entirely relaxed as she munched contentedly, laughing as Suzie alternated between local gossip and comments about the men leaving the toilets.

She looked up as someone approached their table. It was Petra Smith. Petra was the leading figure in the parent's association at Abigail's school. Short, slightly over weight with frizzy ginger hair, she loomed ominously over Jane.

Jane, rather dulled by the wine, smiled up at her. She had always disliked Petra, finding her obsessive organisation rather intimidating. Unless one enjoyed creating models from junk or collecting money from begrudging parents, she was best avoided.

"Hello Jane, I didn't know you came here," stated Petra, as though offended that no one had asked her permission.

"Hi, Petra," drawled Jane, waving a fork in her direction, "how're you?"

"Busy of course, always busy," said Petra, as though there was huge merit in her busyness; as though Jane herself was never busy.

"It's the Summer Fair in two weeks as you know," she said, fairly sure that Jane would have forgotten this important detail. "Have you returned your helpers slip? Not sure that I've seen it. You will help with something wont you? Do your bit? After all, it is our own children who benefit."

Jane vaguely remembered the letter. It had a tear off slip at the bottom, to be returned by the end of the week. There had been a whole list of activities requiring helpers, from stall holders to clearing up afterwards. Jane had used the reverse to write a shopping list. She felt now was not the time to mention this.

170

"Oh yeah." She thought she might be slurring slightly. "I can't think what happened to that. Just put me down for something easy." She paused, trying not to giggle. "I'm a great cook," she added, "maybe I could help with that?"

Petra straightened the sleeves of her trim jacket. She felt there was a joke being played here but was not sure at whom it was aimed. The other woman had clearly been drinking and she was keen to end the conversation. She took a breath.

"Well thank you Jane, I'll add you to the list." She began to back away. "Enjoy your evening," she added uncertainly as Jane was now openly laughing. She fled to join her friends in the restaurant section.

Suzie raised an enquiring eyebrow.

"A mum at Abi's school - PTA," explained Jane. "She's organising the Summer Fete this year. Very bossy."

"And you just volunteered to cook?" queried an amused Suzie. "You? Cook? Oh my!"

Jane giggled and finished the last of her wine.

"Figure she wont ask me again next year. Pudding?"

"Sure. I'll go get the menu. More wine?" Jane gave an affirmative nod. She noticed that her friend had switched to juice but Jane felt she needed to be drunk. She rarely drank, and never more than a small glass. But Peter had forced her here, she was meant to be 'unwinding', having fun. Alcohol might help. Certainly she was feeling happier than she had for months.

She watched the dark oak door that swung heavily to admit new customers, wondering who would emerge. Maybe it would be Matthew, she dreamed, maybe he would join their table, take her home when the evening ended....."

Jane sat up sharply at the sight of the person entering. It was Hilary.

"Oh crap," muttered Jane.

171

Her mother-in-law spotted her instantly and trotted towards her. Her hair was in very stiff curls and Jane guessed that she had spent the afternoon in the hairdressers.

"Jane," called Hilary, "Good evening.

"My daughter-in-law," she explained to her companion, a tall woman in her sixties, dressed in flowing black evening trousers and billowing blouse.

"Having an evening off I see. How nice. Is Peter with you?"

"No," grinned Jane, "I'm here wiv my friend Suzie. Peter's babysitting.

"Suzie, meet Peter's mother," she said, introducing her friend when she arrived. Jane reached for her wine and raised her glass, waving it towards the standing women. "Cheers!"

"Well, I had better find my table. Do take care dear. I think you may have had enough wine for today…"

Jane grinned inanely up at her, not bothering to answer.

She bumped into Hilary again, literally, just before they left. Half a chocolate pudding, more wine and a coffee later, Jane was returning from the Ladies' room. She felt pleasantly fuzzy and was concentrating hard on walking. The floor did not seem to be quite flat. The perimeter of her vision was blurred and she focused on the step in front of her, when her heel turned and she staggered slightly to the side. Hilary happened to be leaving at the same time and was shouldered heavily from the left.

"Oh I say! Jane!" she said, shaken. "Time you went home I think."

"Sorry," mumbled Jane, "it's these heels." She went to meet Suzie.

"Old trout!" she announced in a slightly too loud voice. "I think I might go back and tell her to stop picking on me."

"Maybe now is not the best time," suggested Suzie, as she eased her friend out of the pub and towards the car.

"Hilary!" squealed Jane, "Silly name. Sounds like 'celery'. Hilary Celery. Both are crunchy and rather bitter."

Suzie laughed, "Oh dear, we need to get you home."

Suzie was sober but slightly merry, more catching her mood from Jane than feeling the affects of wine. They drove with the windows down and the music loud. It was very dark and the trees looked ghostly as they were illuminated by the car headlights. Silver grey, they bordered the road on both sides, with only blackness beyond.

Suddenly Suzie stopped the car. They were next to one of the litter signs, its custard yellow paint shining in the dark.

"Do you think it will fit in the boot? I could put it in Nigel's study. Would be *so* funny when he finds it in the morning…"

"*This area is being monitored for litter.*" Jane read slowly through guffaws of laughter. "Let's find out."

The sign was heavier than expected and they had to work together to manoeuvre it into the boot. They had almost accomplished their task when bright headlights approached from behind. They froze, faces turned towards each other, eyes wide.

The approaching lights slowed, almost to a stop. Neither woman breathed. Turned to stone they watched the car in alarm. It drew level with them, yellow lights like great eyes staring at them.

Hilary peered through the night in horror, then, with no expression whatsoever, sped quickly away.

"Oh no! Oh no!" chuckled Jane collapsing in a heap as the red lights disappeared from view. "I will be in such trouble tomorrow."

Tears ran down her cheeks as she gave way to laughter. Suzie hugged her stomach in pain.

"Stop laughing," she pleaded. "It hurts!"

Eventually they managed to stagger back to the car, shut the boot and climb into their seats.

"Quick, drive," instructed Jane, "before she sets the police on us."

"We'll just say we were tidying up," said Suzie, " - taking it home to clean it!"

As Jane kissed her friend goodbye she felt truly happy.

"Thanks Suzie," she said, "that was really fun and I really enjoyed it."

She walked carefully to the front door and spent a few minutes trying to fit the key into the lock before she was able to enter.

Voices drifted from the lounge. Frowning, she walked to the room and found Peter and Abigail watching a film. Peter smiled, Abigail looked guilty.

"Daddy said I could stay up and watch this," she declared, defensive as she saw her mother's expression.

"Yes," said Peter, "she helped me get Chris to sleep so I said she could." He glanced at the clock. "I didn't realise it was quite so late though young lady. Better scoot!"

Abigail kissed him quickly and looked at her mother. She did not read great affection in her expression, so waved apologetically and slipped past her to the safety of the hall. She could hear her voice, cross and accusing:

"Honestly Peter, I leave you to sort out the kids for one night. One night! Now she'll be all tired and grumpy tomorrow. It's alright for you, it's me who'll suffer."

"Nice evening?" he enquired obtusely.

She glared at him.

"I'm going to bed," she said.

"Yes, you do that," she heard him mutter. "Don't bother to thank me for babysitting so you could go out."

She stamped up the stairs, noticing tea things still on the table through the open kitchen door. Christopher's clothes left a trail across the landing, as though he had been rugby tackled out of them. She could hear a tap dripping in the bathroom.

Reaching her room, she slumped on the bed. The window was open and a fly whined around the lamp. She sighed. All the laughter and happiness had seeped out of her. She felt empty again, cross and tired. She didn't know why she should be made to feel guilty for having left the children with Peter - they were after all, his children too. It was his house, his mess, his family. Why should it all be dumped on Jane all the time? Noticing the beginnings of a headache, she went to remove her make-up.

Chapter Eighteen

The following Thursday, Jane took Christopher to the park. It was a beautiful Summer's day, with a high blue sky and a gentle breeze. She had parked in the small car park near the swings, and now they walked hand in hand across the grass. Max was in an ecstasy of sniffing under a wooden bench. The sun glinted off the paint of the large red slide and Christopher was skipping at her side. Her bag bumped against her hip. She needed to buy white cotton on the way home so that she could reattach buttons to Abigail's school blouse.

School was not a happy thought at the moment. She had been summarily telephoned following her evening out and told: thank you for volunteering, you are manning the barbecue at the Summer Fair. Burgers! It was bad enough having to cook at home, now she would be burning food for the whole school. She sighed, at least she had nothing to prepare and it was only one day.

She lifted Christopher onto a swing and pulled it back. It was wooden and heavy, with a thick metal chain. She released it, watching it swing free, then braced for its return. Christopher wiggled his legs.

"Higher! Higher!" he chanted.

"That's enough Chris," she sighed after a few minutes. "You play on the roundabout, I need to find Max."

She left her son climbing onto the orange wheel and went in search of the dog. He lumbered over when she called, tail swaying, stick in mouth. She obediently threw the stick a few times, watching her son as he played in the low fenced enclosure. He too had found a stick and was poking beneath the roundabout. She walked over to where he was.

Red faced and frowning he was peering under the roundabout, making frantic sweeps with a thin branch.

176

"I can nearly get it," he said in frustration.

At last, with one long swoosh of the stick, his prize was dislodged and tumbled over the grass in the sunlight.

"It's magic!" he cried.

"It's dirty!" she said.

It was a whiskey bottle, drained empty and flung under the child's toy with drunken disregard. The golden label sparkled in the sunlight enticingly. Before she could stop him, Christopher had snatched it up.

"Can I keep it?"

"No," said his mother, "it's got germs on it. Don't touch it."

The boy inspected it closely. No germs could be seen. The glass was very smooth and the lid was made of gold. The label was beautiful and seemed to have secret writing on it. It was clearly magic. He glanced at his mother. Her face looked cross and he could tell she did not understand the importance of his treasure. He felt his bottom lip begin to quiver.

"Please mummy, it's mine now."

Jane looked into the deep pools of his pleading eyes. 'How am I supposed to not give in?' she wondered. She knelt down and put an arm around his narrow shoulders. He gazed trustingly at her.

"Chris, it's not clean," she began. His eyes began to fill with tears. "Alright, we can take it home and wash it I suppose."

She removed it from his grasp, deciding it would be easily disposed of later, when he had forgotten about it. She called the dog and clipped on his lead, then told Christopher that they needed to buy cotton before they went home. Not having a hand free to hold his, she sighed and slipped the bottle into her bag, hoping it was not as dirty as she feared.

They moved to the road and stood waiting as traffic passed. Jane watched the cars impatiently, wanting to go home.

177

Suddenly, with heart lurching familiarly, she recognised Matthew's car. He glided down the road towards her. She searched for his face. He saw her, raised a hand in salute and continued past.

"That was Matfew!" announced Christopher.

"Yes," said Jane, watching the car until it disappeared.

"Mummy, we can go," said Christopher, waggling her hand so that she would notice the road was clear. Trance like she led him across.

She was a blur of emotion. She had seen him. He had waved. Their contact was not completely severed. Maybe she would see him again one day. Perhaps, now he knew they visited the park sometimes he would drive past again.

Or perhaps not.

She took a deep breath and gave herself a mental shake. This was silly. She was like a teenager with a crush on a celebrity. This obsession was getting out of hand.

"Come along," she said and led the way to the hardware shop.

#

Leaving the dog tied miserably to the post outside, they entered the gloom of the shop. It smelt of glue and fabric. The floor was grey cement and the air felt cold after the warmth of outside. Narrow aisles were precariously stacked to the ceiling with a jumble of products.

"Don't touch anything," Jane instructed.

She led him past cans of paint, a display of brushes perched above an array of door locks. Helpful signs warned of guard dogs, not to park in front of entrances and a request to close the gate. Christopher put out a finger and traced their cold letters. They walked around stacked plastic buckets, and passed mops that bent shaggy heads towards them. His finger trailed across rough doormats and onto shiny saucepans that stood in pyramids above his head. They passed boxes of electrical appliances, which nestled

178

against a display of scissors. Bolts of coloured fabric were piled almost to the ceiling. He reached out and stroked pink fur, then poked a finger through some white lace.

"You're touching!" his mother hissed, "Fold your arms."

She had stopped beside a rack of coloured cottons. Selecting a reel of white, she guided him back towards the door to pay.

The counter was very high, much taller than his head. Behind it was a tiny man with a white beard. Christopher was fairly sure he was an elf. His mother seemed to have not noticed, and was searching for her purse. He moved behind her. There was an interesting display of tools hanging from the wall. Bright orange handles with comfortable grips, connected to grim looking blades. Saws of various sizes hung like crocodile jaws. He reached out a hand. His mother was busy paying. He pointed a finger and ran it along a blade. He snatched back his hand. Dark red blood oozed through his fist. It stung. He screamed.

"Mummy!"

Jane turned. She heard the cry, turned while pulling her purse from her bag, saw the blood and leapt towards her child. Off balance, her foot caught on the edge of a broom, which began to tumble, bringing another broom with it. She tripped. As she fell, she put out a hand to save herself, pulling a large tin of emulsion to the concrete with her. Jane, brooms, a brush and the tin all fell to the floor with a crash.

For a long second, all was still. Jane was lying on the floor; Christopher standing above her, his crying suspended; the shopkeeper, watching.

Then they all moved as one. Christopher began to wail and Jane sat up, opening her arms for him. The shopkeeper hurried towards them, full of defensive concern.

"Madam, you really shouldn't let your little boy touch things," he clucked anxiously.

179

Jane ignored him and inspected the wound. It was very minor and had stopped bleeding already. She put his finger in her mouth and sucked to clean the wound. Then she wiped his tears with her fingers and kissed his nose.

"Stop crying, you're alright," she said quietly, reassuring him.

"It bit me," he whispered.

Jane smiled, "You shouldn't have touched."

"I do think you should watch him more closely in future," said the shopkeeper. "This is not a toy shop."

Jane declined to comment and began to get up off the floor. All was fine until she put weight on her right ankle. Pain shot up her leg. She sat again quickly, waves of nausea washing over her.

"Are you alright?" asked the man. "You really should have looked where you were going. Luckily I do not believe anything was damaged, so I wont have to charge you."

He picked up a couple of brooms and replaced them on the stand then retrieved the paint.

"It's lucky this lid stayed on," he said. "You would have made no end of mess if that had come off. You cant rely on that you know. Manufacturers do not guarantee that lids won't come loose. Paint should always be stored upright you know."

He paused.

The woman was still sitting on his floor. She did seem rather pale. He did hope she would not faint. It would not be good for business.

"I'm afraid I need you to move," he said, his voice rising a pitch. "I will have other customers shortly and you are rather in the way."

'Customers,' he thought, 'who will buy more than a single reel of cotton and who will create a lot less fuss.'

Jane remained on the floor. She really was unsure if she could stand. Her ankle hurt a huge amount and she felt quite ill with pain.

Then, as if she were in some ludicrous farce, the shop door opened and in walked Hilary.

Her gaze swept across the tear stained child, the flustered shopkeeper and Jane, who was sitting on the floor.

"And what happened here?" she asked.

"This woman did not have her child under appropriate control and he handled the merchandise" the man hurried to explain. "Then she did not give due care and attention to her actions and she fell over. Nearly damaging more goods, may I add."

"I see," said Hilary. "Jane, can you stand?"

"It hurts," said Jane, "I don't know." She looked at the shopkeeper. "Do you have a stick I could lean on?"

"She could purchase a walking stick," he informed Hilary, deciding that Jane was best not spoken to and realising the two women were acquainted.

"Right, please fetch one," the older woman commanded, "and Christopher, please sit on this chair and hold my handbag with both hands."

Christopher obeyed. He was reassured by her presence, and now she was clearly in charge of the situation he was extremely interested to see what would happen. His finger only hurt a little bit now, the pain eclipsed by the excitement of seeing Jane on the floor. He wondered if Nana would tell her off for getting dirty. He clutched the bulky bag. It was shiny black leather and very full. He longed to peek inside and investigate the contents but felt sure someone would then tell *him* off. Instead he held it close to his chest, feeling the hard shapes inside. He found he could make his finger bleed again if he pressed it very hard, and he amused himself creating a line of round red spots across the width of the bag.

The man reappeared with a selection of sticks.

181

"Which would madam prefer? Lightweight steel or more traditional wood? Or perhaps one with a seat incorporated into the handle?"

Hilary pointed at a wooden stick with a plain curved handle.

"That one is suitable," she said. She looked at Jane, "You can reimburse me later." She handed her credit card to the shopkeeper.

They both helped Jane to stand and she tested her weight on the stick. She could walk, but it was painful. Driving would be difficult, so Hilary agreed that she would drive them all home. When she realised that a dog was involved she bought a long length of thick polythene. She then spent several minutes lining the footwell of her car while Jane sat awkwardly in the shop, Christopher standing close.

Jane thanked the shopkeeper uncertainly.

"Yes, he responded, "well, I hope this has been a lesson to you, young lady. One needs to take more care in life if one is not going to be an inconvenience. Perhaps you will take better care of your child in future."

The child in question gave him an angelic smile, and placed a tenth bloody fingerprint on an unseen white tea towel before following his mother out of the shop.

Hilary had driven round to the shop front, so Jane had to hobble only as far as the curb. She lowered herself into the passenger seat. Christopher climbed in beside her. There was no child seat, which worried Jane, but she decided the journey was short enough to merit risking an adult's seat belt. She pushed her coat under him, to act as a booster seat. Hilary, sighing loudly, was loading the dog.

They drove to Jane's house in near silence. At one point she tried to thank her mother-in-law and explain what had happened. Hilary waved a hand dismissively. Jane was unsure if this was at the thanks or the explanation.

When they arrived, Hilary leant across for Jane's bag.

"Let me take that for you," she said, "then I can unlock the front door and come back to help you."

She walked down the path then stood by the door and unzipped the bag. There, at the top, was a bottle. Slowly she removed it. A whiskey bottle. An empty whiskey bottle. Her daughter-in-law had been at the park with a bottle of whiskey, and then had fallen over. She looked back at the car. Mother and child were both watching her. With a frown she found the keys and unlocked the door.

"I think this discussion is best kept for another time," she decided, placing the bag on the hall table. Then she went back to help Jane.

Later, Jane sat on the sofa sipping tea. Hilary had advised her to bind the ankle tightly, cover it with a bag of frozen peas and raise it on a cushion. She had collected Abigail from school and offered to help the following day if necessary.

"I hope it wont be necessary," thought Jane, "I feel such an inconvenience when she helps me."

She smiled at the memory of her unexpected appearance. Then her thoughts wandered to her glimpse of Matthew.

"Of all the moments when he could have passed," she thought, "it was just as we were crossing. It's like it was fate, like our paths were meant to cross." It was a comforting idea and she settled against the cushions. "I wish I could tell him what happened," she yearned. "He would laugh with me, make me feel better about that horrible man.

"There's no one to tell," she realised. "Peter will just tell me I'm silly, and then rush to thank Hilary. Once he's spoken to her, he'll be convinced I'm inadequate. They will make me feel like it was my fault, they won't be sympathetic. He never sides with me against his mother. He won't defend me to her, he won't laugh about her with me. I am the outsider."

A shot of loneliness pierced her and she felt close to tears.

"Oh Matthew, I do miss you," she thought, "when will I see you again…?"

Chapter Nineteen

The day of the Summer Fete arrived all too quickly. Jane was cooking with two other mothers. She recognised their names but did not really know them. She had been told that everything would be provided, she just had to bring an apron.

Peter promised to take good care of Christopher and Abigail. He planned to bring them both later and was now busy sorting money. He had emptied a huge jar of loose change, collected over several months, onto the table.

"Good opportunity this," he remarked cheerily, making piles of pennies and two pence pieces, then putting them into sandwich bags when he had a pound of each.

Jane eyed the mass of coppers dubiously. She was not entirely sure that a pounds worth of pennies would be welcome at each stall. She decided not to comment and rummaged in a drawer for an apron. It was green and flowery and had a hard lump of old pastry stuck to the pocket. She was late, it would have to do. She said goodbye and left.

#

The barbecue pitch was in the corner of the playground, next to an inflated pool of floating ducks. The ducks had small rings attached to their backs, ready for young children to fish them out with hooked poles. Many of them were floating upside down and a rather harried mother was attempting to readjust their weights. It was not an easy task and the yellow ducks persisted in floating with their silly faces submerged. A football bounced across the playground and landed in the pool. The mother glowered damply. It was followed across the tarmac by a bouncy father.

"Sorry," he yelled happily. "Nice warm day to get splashed though. I'll return this to the 'Beat the Goalie' stall - maybe we should rename it '*Beat the Ducks*.' Ha!"

He retrieved his ball and bounded away. Jane heard dark mutterings from the duck lady and smiled. She was busy weighting down paper napkins and plates on a table. It was breezy and they fluttered as though trying to escape. There were several bottles of tomato sauce - the cheap runny stuff that tastes of acidic sugar, and a fat tube of mustard. She left her task and went to find the meat.

Sausages and burgers were stored in cool boxes beside the barbecues. Jane was working with May and Alice. Both wore smart navy and white striped aprons, and were brisk and well organised. May had attached the gas to the barbecues and was now heating them. Alice was deciding how much meat to cook initially.

"You do the sausages Jane," said Alice, glad to have someone to organise. "Start with about thirty and see how you get on. The barbecues should be ready in about ten minutes."

Jane began counting sausages, pulling them from the the box in strings.

"What are you doing?" asked May.

"Getting them ready..." hesitated Jane.

"Oh. Well, you could separate them I suppose" said May, sounding doubtful. "It is much too early to start cooking them though. And do try and keep them off the cloth, we need to keep raw meat away from where we'll be serving. Obviously."

"Obviously," agreed Jane, coiling the string of meat onto a plate. She needed to separate them, but wasn't sure how. Frozen sausages were already separated. She didn't have a knife. She took the first sausage and pulled hard. It slithered, greasy, in her hand, depositing a blob of sausage meat on the tablecloth.

"Here." May passed her a knife. Jane cut through the skin.

"You need to prick those," said Alice.

"No, it's best not to," contradicted May.

Jane had no opinion at all, so covered them with a napkin and went to wash her hands.

To the left of the barbecue was a trestle table laden with mouldering books. The covers were faded and the pages brown, many showing unevenly at the sides where they had come away from their binding. Jane recognised some titles from the book stall at the Christmas Fair. The parent manning the stall was making neat piles of adult books, with children's titles spread out at the front. He surreptitiously sidled one back into the box. Jane wondered if the title was deemed too racy or if he fancied reading it himself.

She passed a tombola, a bouncy castle, and a table spread with a treasure island. There was a candy-floss seller, signs beckoning her to guess the weight, guess the name and have a lucky dip. One mother had dressed as a gypsy with red headscarf and hooped earrings, and was offering to read palms. Another was busy arranging face paints on a small table.

There was a cake stall, laden with sponges sweating in cellophane and plates of smaller cakes ready to be eaten. Someone was unloading two grumpy donkeys from a horse box. Jane could hear the chairman of the governors testing the microphone as she entered the school and went in search of the girl's toilets.

#

When she emerged from the school, people were beginning to arrive. Excited children hurried through the gate, followed by cautious parents who stopped to pay their one pound entrance fee and collect a photocopied programme.

"Where have you been?" said Alice, as Jane arrived back at the stall.

"She washed her hands," said May.

"Oh. We can't keep disappearing," said Alice, frowning. "Here!" She handed Jane a pack of disinfectant hand wipes.

187

"Of course," said May, "those are only good for killing germs on clean hands. They will not actually remove any dirt. Proper dirt needs to be washed away with soapy water."

"Better start cooking," said Alice, ignoring her.

"Probably better to wait a while," decided May. "We'll begin in ten minutes." She looked at her watch, as if absorbing the time.

Jane decided not to point out that ten minutes would make very little difference. She spied Peter coming through the gate. He held a purple carrier bag and was laboriously counting pennies into the patient hand of the parent on the gate.

He saw her and hurried over. Alice and May were busy, placing meat on the barbecues.

"We made it!" said Peter, as if this was unexpected. He was not often in sole charge of the children.

"Yes, well done," said Jane. She moved closer, "You will keep an eye on Christopher wont you? Don't let him wander off on his own.

"Abi does country dancing at two, so she'll need to change into plimsolls before then. Listen for the announcement."

"We'll be fine," said Peter. "We're raring to go, aren't we Chris?"

Christopher grinned up at his father. He was clutching an orange bag, which Jane feared was also full of pennies.

"Don't let them eat too many sweets," she pleaded. "And definitely nothing that's not wrapped." She lowered her voice again. "Some of the little cakes look a bit dodgy," she said, "can you make sure the kids don't buy them?"

"We'll be fine," repeated Peter. "Come on Chris, donkey ride I think before the queue gets any longer."

Jane watched them walk away, then turned to the sausages and began to add them to the barbecue.

#

188

There was little time for conscious thought for the rest of the afternoon. The women had a steady stream of customers at their stall and Jane worked hard, turning sausages, placing them on the outstretched rolls, turning down the heat to a mere glow.

May was busy with burgers, flipping them every few minutes, then turning to check Jane's progress with the sausages.

"These are a bit slow," she said, worried, turning the heat up to full. "They need to be cooked quickly."

Jane passed a sausage to a waiting child. Alice fished for change in her money pot. Then she moved back to check the meat.

"We don't want them to cook on the outside before the middle is heated through," she said, turning the heat back down to its lowest setting.

Jane saw Abigail arriving, laden with bottles.

"Dad's on the tombola," she informed Jane, passing her some olive oil and bright green bubble bath.

"It takes him ages to count out the money," she giggled. "Can you hold these?"

Jane bent and hid them under the table. May leant over her and turned up the heat on the barbecue.

"Don't forget it's country dancing later," said Jane, as Abigail skipped away. She returned to the sausages. A few were beginning to turn black.

"You must keep turning them," chided May.

"That heat's too high," observed Alice, reaching to turn it down.

Jane began to slice a fresh batch of finger rolls. Abigail returned, this time carrying a bottle of rum and some cheap red wine.

"Dad says his luck is improving," she told Jane, passing her the bottles.

"You can't keep those here," said Alice, "they'll be in the way."

"I thought they could go under the table," said Jane.

Alice and May exchanged looks. Either one was helping to run a stall, or one was not. Bottles were an unnecessary hindrance. They said nothing. They didn't need to, their expressions were eloquent.

Jane paused.

"They can go in your locker Abi," she decided, "we can get them later." She passed them back to her daughter.

"And don't run with them!" she called, as Abigail hurried towards the school with her latest prizes.

May turned down the heat on both barbecues and began to move the cooked sausages to the edge. Jane handed two sausages to a parent, then tried to open a new sauce bottle. The foil seal under the lid was firmly stuck down and she could not lift it. She scratched at it for a while, then grabbed a fork and stabbed through it. Red sauce squirted out, splattering her fingers and the table.

"Well that's one way of doing it," said a familiar voice. Jane whirled around. There, standing behind her, was Matthew.

He stood close, smiling down at her. Jane felt herself blush with surprise as she returned his smile.

"What…?" she began.

"I saw the posters," explained Matthew, "wondered if you'd be here. Though not," he admitted, "at this particular stall. Cooking...?" He raised an eyebrow.

Jane laughed, her heart singing. The whole world felt brighter.

"Be careful, or I'll sauce you!" she threatened, wiggling her red coated fingers towards his face.

"I need to wash these," she said, and began to walk towards the school, ignoring Alice as she waved wet wipes at her.

Matthew followed, chatting easily. She didn't look at him, but was aware of his proximity, aware that he was with her.

They went into the school, gloomy after the brightness of the sunny afternoon. The corridor was deserted, everyone outside at the stalls. Their footsteps sounded loud in the quiet building, it felt forbidden to be inside, as if they were breaking some rule. Still Jane did not look at him. She could feel her heart, was very aware of everything, especially how alone they were. How unseen.

They reached the sinks, and she paused. She looked at her hands, red with sauce. Matthew reached down, over her, to turn on the tap for her. He was leaning very close, looking at her face. She could smell him now, that soapy smell she knew so well. She opened her mouth to thank him for turning on the tap.

"I missed you!" she blurted out, the tension of the moment controlling her words.

She was immediately mortified. What would he think of her? He would think she was some desperate, clingy housewife. She felt her face burn and thrust her hands under the water, washing them frantically, wondering what she could say to make it sound less odd, less blunt. Trying to make the moment casual, like it didn't really matter.

"Hey," he said softly, seeing her confusion. He was still looking at her, trying to read her expression. "I missed you too," he said, trying to take the tension from the exchange, to stop her embarrassment. "I used to enjoy chatting with you," he said, "we had fun didn't we?"

Jane nodded. She wanted so badly to salvage the situation, to turn this back into a light conversation between casual friends. But he was too close. She was too aware of him.

He paused, as though considering an idea. He moved even closer, they were almost touching, and when he spoke, Jane could feel his breath on her cheek. She thought, for one wild moment, that he might be going to kiss her.

"We could meet, if you want," he murmured, so quietly that Jane could hardly hear him. He was still looking at her, an intense stare, holding her eyes with his own, seeing, Jane felt, into the depths of her.

She nodded, not trusting herself to speak. The corridor where they stood felt full of electricity. Jane broke his gaze and looked around. The sink had splatters of powder paint around the edges and smelt of damp newspaper. Everything looked normal. Nothing had changed.

She shook the drips from her fingers and turned off the tap.

"Okay," he said. He reached up, tucked a stray hair behind her ear. Jane thought she might melt. She kept very still, not daring to breathe. Something had changed between them, unspoken but tangible.

"I'll text you, in a few days, arrange something?" he said, raising an eyebrow.

Jane nodded, smiling now.

"I'd better go," he said, "can I trust you not to kill anyone with that sauce bottle?"

The tension was gone, they were back in familiar territory.

"I think so," grinned Jane.

She watched him leave. She stood at the small children's sink, and watched this man, this man who she desired, as he walked the length of the corridor. Tall, broad shouldered, moving with fluid ease, looking as out of place in a primary school as a film star. Then through the door, and he was gone.

She dried her hands on the rough green paper towel and dropped it into the open bin beside the sink.

"He came to see me." Her thoughts were a whirl, tumbling in a muddle with her emotions.

"He still has my mobile number," she realised. "He wants to see me. It was his idea, he suggested it, he wants to see me. I matter."

Feeling somewhat shell shocked, she returned to her stall. Along the corridor, back into the sunlight. No sign of him now, as she passed the cake stall, the books, parents queuing at the tombola. She walked, dream-like, through the crowd. Nothing felt real, it was as if Jane had evaporated, and some shell, which looked exactly like Jane, was now acting in her place. She was behaving like the old Jane, she spoke and responded like the old Jane, but it was all pretend. Jane, the real Jane, was somewhere else.

Several customers were waiting for sausages. Alice had taken their money but felt unable to serve them - for health and safety reasons, she explained. One should not handle both money and food. May had disappeared to use the toilet.

Jane screwed the lid onto the rather sticky sauce bottle and reached for the tongs. She lifted the sausages onto the waiting rolls with a polite smile, apologising for the delay.

Abigail appeared. She pushed her way through the queue.

"I've lost a plimsoll," she announced.

Jane stopped, feeling confused, sausage suspended in mid air.

"He must like me, really like me," she had been thinking, "to risk coming to a school fair."

"What?" she asked, slightly dazed.

"My plimsoll," repeated Abigail loudly. "I have lost my plimsoll. And I need it for dancing. Now!"

Jane became aware of the voice crackling from the loud speaker.

"Could all our dancers please join Miss Mott next to class four, for the country dancing."

"Oh, I see," said Jane.

193

"It should be in my locker," said Abigail, growing more agitated, "someone has stolen it."

"I expect it's there somewhere," mumbled Jane, wondering if she could abandon Alice again to help her daughter. However, the decision was unnecessary as Hilary and George appeared in the centre of the playground.

"There's Gran!" said Abigail, "She can help."

She ran across to her grandparents, who looked relieved to see her.

"Ah, Abigail," said Hilary, "we were wondering where you were. Your father said to come at two o'clock."

"And we were here on time," added George.

"I've lost a plimsoll," Abigail said, "and I need it for country dancing, which is now. Can you help me find it? - Please," she added, as an after thought.

"Can't you dance in shoes?" asked George. "It's only skipping really."

"Oh George, of course she can't," said Hilary. "Right, you go and find Peter," she said to her husband. "Abigail, show me where your gym shoe *should* be, we'll start there."

"Plimsoll," corrected Abigail as she led her grandmother into the school.

They passed a mother and child as they left the toilets but the rest of the corridor was empty. It seemed strangely dim without the strip lighting turned on and Abigail felt it was a little frightening being here alone. Her grandmother's heels clicked authoritatively beside her as they walked past giant collages of multi coloured birds.

They went to the cloakroom and she pointed to her locker. It was a red cubbyhole, one of several against the wall opposite the coat pegs. There was a number six painted above it.

"That's mine," she said, "but no plimsoll."

Hilary opened the door, and decided the best method would be to empty it completely. It had the look of a cupboard that had been rummaged through. She began to remove items and pass them to Abigail. Navy blue shorts were tangled with a white tee shirt.

"That's what we wear for PE," said Abigail, being helpful. There was a pink folder with torn covers. "That's History." Next came a black plimsoll, with a white sock tucked inside. "That's the one I already found," she said, folding her arms.

Then, jammed safely at the back, were two bottles. The rum was standing upright, its lid nearly touching the top of the locker. The wine was on its side, wedged with a sock and a sweatshirt.

"Those are Mummy's," said Abigail. "She'll get them later I expect."

Hilary paused, said nothing. Instead, she knelt down and felt beneath the unit. Her hand closed around a soft shoe. She extracted the rather dusty plimsoll and handed it to Abigail, who beamed at her.

"Just in time!" she said, pushing it onto her foot.

"Thanks Gran," she called as she ran back to the playground. Hilary folded the clothes and placed them tidily in the locker before closing the door and returning to her husband.

#

George was standing with Peter and Christopher on the edge of a ring of parents. A large space had been cleared in the centre of the playground and the first class was skipping in pairs to their starting positions. Music, slightly off-key, was blaring from the loud speaker and a teacher was gesticulating wildly, trying to encourage the children to smile. They frowned back at her as they stood in lines, waiting to begin.

Jane hurried over as the dance started.

"You smell of sausage," said Peter.

"Why is Chris eating a fairy cake?" hissed Jane. "You don't know how many people have breathed on that. He'll be ill."

"He'll be fine," said Peter. "Look, here comes Abi. Dances like a donkey!"

It seemed to Jane that the dancing lasted a very long time. It consisted primarily of skipping in a circle, with the odd exchange of partner along the way. The music was unpleasant and jarred her nerves. Most parents were clapping enthusiastically whilst staring with unseeing eyes.

"What is this dance?" queried Hilary, "I don't recognise it."

"Gay Gordons, I think," said Peter.

"Well, they are doing it wrong," observed Hilary.

"Perhaps they tried to simplify it," said Peter.

"No," she said, "it's not simplified, it's just wrong. And that boy has his shoes on the wrong feet. I'm very surprised his teacher didn't make him change them."

"Perhaps she didn't notice," said George.

"It's her job to notice," stated Hilary.

"This music is giving me a headache," complained George. "Can't they turn it down a bit?"

Jane, who until this moment had also found it unpleasantly loud, felt irritated.

"I like it," she said, "it's happy." She began to clap with renewed vigour. The children continued to skip, some of them frowning with concentration, some smiling at their parents. A few looked as bored as the audience.

"I might," began Christopher, pulling at her sleeve with sticky fingers, "I might, be going to wet myself."

"Right," said Jane, glad to escape, "let's go quickly. Hold it in until we get there."

They pushed through the crowd and hurried into the school.

"Hold it in, hold it in," chanted Christopher, enjoying the echo of the corridor. "Hold it in!"

They arrived in time. Jane rushed to wash his hands and get back to the dancing before she missed her daughter. She felt cross, now she thought about it, that Hilary had let her take Christopher rather than offering to help so that Jane could watch the dancing.

In the playground, Abigail was doing her final courtesy. She grinned up at her mother in triumph. Jane waved and passed Christopher back to Peter. He was chewing a hot dog.

"Bit crisp," he said, "but edible."

"I think we've finished," said Jane, "I'd better help clear up. Can you take the kids?"

"Sure," mumbled Peter through a mouthful of sausage.

#

Alice and May were removing the last pieces of meat from the barbecues. Alice flapped the wet wipes at Jane as she approached.

"Health and safety," she said.

Jane failed to see how it mattered as they were clearing up but she wiped her hands obediently.

"We need to cool these grills and then scrub them," said May.

"No," said Alice, "better to shut them and turn up the gas to full. Burn off all the fat."

Jane returned the bread rolls to their bags and began throwing away soiled napkins.

"I'll count the money," offered Alice. "It will take me a long time, thanks to that man."

"Yes," said May, her voice outraged, "while you were gone Jane, a father bought three hot dogs and paid for them in pennies."

"Pennies!" repeated Alice, "Pennies! Can you imagine how long it will take me to count them all? Never mind the weight!"

"Thoughtless," said May.

"Very," agreed Alice.

197

"Oh well," thought Jane, "at least they agree on something."
She decided not to reply.

#

By the time they had cleared up, most people had left. Peter
wandered over to say that they were leaving and would see Jane
when she got home. She nodded, pushing a paper table covering
into a too full dustbin liner.

"Wait!" said Christopher, "My stuff - we mustn't forget my
stuff."

"Oh yes," said Abigail, "he did vey well."

He ran back towards a nearly empty stall and heaved two big
bags from underneath.

"I gave him some money," said Peter.

"He got some real bargains," added Abigail proudly.

Jane's heart sank. She knew from previous fetes that the
second-hand toy stall was always left with broken, dirty toys.
Things that people had discarded but did not want to throw away
were regularly dumped at school fairs. Now, as she watched her
son struggle excitedly towards her, she knew that much of this
rubbish was heading towards her home. The mother manning the
stall was sweeping up, determinedly not looking at Jane. She
sighed.

"I'll see them at home," she said.

#

As she finally drove away from the school, Jane felt tired. It had
been a busy day, but mainly emotionally draining. A new knot had
formed in her stomach and she could feel the tension in her
muscles.

"Matthew."

She wondered when he would contact her, where they would
meet. She felt excited, but not, if she were honest with herself,

198

particularly happy. She knew there were thoughts at the back of her mind that she was refusing to face.

"I don't need to think about this," she decided, "I'll just wait and see what happens." She arrived home and opened the door. Grubby toys were strewn across the floor. Odd jigsaw pieces lay next to a doll's head beside a plastic castle which was missing a turret.

Jane stepped carefully into the kitchen.

"I need tea," she said. Peter looked up and grinned at her. He was at the kitchen table, reading the front of the local newspaper. He looked rather pleased with himself.

"Chris is happy," he said. "Oh, and this came for you."

It was a plain white envelope with her name handwritten across the front. She did not recognise the writing, nor was she expecting anything. She froze. Peter was watching her curiously. Was it from Matthew? Was it possible that he had gone to text her, realised he had deleted her number, and had written her a note instead? Would he be that stupid?

"I'll open it later," she said, keeping her voice flippant and filling the kettle with an unsteady hand, "I need some tea first."

"Poor old thing," smiled Peter. "Here, you sit down and open your letter, I'll make the tea."

Jane slumped in a chair. Peter was watching her, she didn't really have a choice. She felt nauseous as she slowly tore the envelope, something cold and hard spreading through her stomach. Every nerve was screaming and she felt like her blood carried shards of ice. For the first time in her life she knew what it was to feel frightened. Peter, the boy she had married, laughed with, shared her life with; in one simple stroke, he turned from her best friend to her enemy. Instead of wanting to share everything, she wanted to hide, to deceive him.

"Actually, I'm desperate for the loo," she said, standing up. "Be back in a minute". She hurried from the room, knocking her elbow on the doorframe as she left, crumpling the letter in her hand as if distracted.

In the safety of the bathroom, with the door locked, she perched on the toilet and finished opening the envelope. She peered inside. There appeared to be a printed leaflet. Frowning, she slid it from the envelope.

"Alcoholics Anonymous" was the title. It was a small printed tract, giving venues and times of their meetings. Someone had printed her name across the top.

"I don't understand," she said, confusion replacing her fear. She stood, her heart rate returning to normal, unlocked the door, and went back to the kitchen. She showed the pamphlet to Peter.

"I don't know why I've been sent this," she said. "It's got my name on it, so it can't be a mistake."

"Probably someone wants you to go and help," suggested Peter, turning to make the tea.

The door opened and Christopher appeared. He took a hesitant step towards his mother and paused. She rose hurriedly to meet him.

"I feel..." he began. Then was promptly sick all over the floor.

Jane shut her eyes for two seconds, then with a deep breath she moved to carry him upstairs.

Chapter Twenty

They carried their coffee outside to some shiny metal chairs and placed it gingerly on a small round table that wobbled. Had they been more practical, thought Jane, they would have fiddled with folded paper and matchboxes until they had a suitable wedge to solve the problem. Instead, they sat carefully and held their coffees with both hands. The cups were large, more like bowls and were heavy to lift. There was something incongruous about sitting in the middle of a High Street, as though pretending they were in the South of France, with neither the scenery nor the relaxed pace. However, the day was sunny and warm and it was not an unpleasant place to be.

Jane was almost bursting with her news and she launched into it.

"I met Matthew," she told Suzie.

"Matthew?" frowned Suzie, "The labourer?"

This irritated Jane. He was not a 'labourer', he was a perfectly intelligent human and he was her friend. She found the description demeaning.

"The guy who built our extension, yes. I met him by chance but he suggested that we meet up sometime."

"*We* being just you, or you *and* Peter?" asked Suzie.

"Me," said Jane, "I hardly think Peter would approve. He has his own friends, anyway - all the people at work."

Suzie balanced her coffee back on the saucer and looked hard at her friend. She was not quite sure what she was being told.

"And where is this going to lead?" said Suzie, "What are you planning will happen?"

"I don't know," admitted Jane. She leant forwards and confided in a low voice, "And I don't care. It's exciting. It makes me happy just thinking about it."

She sat back, satisfied. She had been longing to tell Suzie and so had arranged to meet her for coffee. She was certain her friend, ever fun loving, would be captivated by the story, and had looked forward to confiding, laughing, making plans together. She was also hoping for a reliable alibi should the need arise.

The two women had been friends for years, meeting at antenatal classes when expecting their sons. It had been an easy friendship, rooted in those early weeks of motherhood when even combing their hair had been a task to remember. They had worried together before labour, wept together through sheer exhaustion after sleepless nights and shared potty training traumas. The bond was deep. Jane felt that anyone willing to befriend you during those emotionally turbulent months when you resembled a slug and smelt of cheese, was a friend indeed.

"I think, " she whispered, "that I am possibly going to have an affair." She waited, smiling.

"Think?" queried Suzie, with narrowed eyes.

"Well," admitted Jane, "nothing has happened yet." She replaced her cup on the swaying table and resumed her story.

"You must remember Matthew," she urged, wondering why her friend wasn't eating up this delicious piece of news. Suzie nodded and she continued in a rush. "Well, I've been thinking about him loads, couldn't stop. And I really missed him when he left, felt sort of lonely. We'd become friends you see. He's not just a *labourer,* he's intelligent and funny, and we shared - I don't know - a connection I guess. We talked a lot. All the time really," she swallowed. "Then I saw him again at the Summer Fete. I think maybe he came specially, looking for me. And we chatted a bit and then he suggested that we meet somewhere. And I think it means that he's interested in me. That perhaps we could continue the relationship…"

She trailed off uncertainly. Suzie's face was hard. She was silent for a long time, just looking at Jane.

"You'll be a bloody fool if you do!" she said at last. Her voice was quiet, but the intensity shook Jane.

She was shocked. She had been sure that Suzie would share her secret with delight. She was always playful, loved to be outrageous and laughed easily. It was not like her to be strict or moralising. She had thought her friend would want to be involved in this game, would share the fun of it, would be on Jane's side.

Suzie sipped her coffee.

"It's up to you, I guess," she said at last. "We are, after all, the generation of choice. We all got an education, we can decide if we want to work, if and when we want children. We all think we've got a God-given right to happiness and fulfilment, don't we?" Suzie sat straighter, warming to her theme, deciding to be honest with her friend. "Well, I for one don't think we do, not really, not if it means hurting other people. That's what animals do, not people, not grown-ups." She took a sip of coffee, allowing herself time to think, to plan her attack.

"Did you love Peter, really love him, when you got married?"

Jane nodded. This was going horribly wrong, she had not intended to be lectured.

"And does he hit you?" asked Suzie, "Abuse the kids? Keep you locked up? Mentally torture you?"

"Well, no," admitted Jane, "but there is Izzy..."

"Oh bollocks!" declared Suzie. "You don't know for sure that anything's going on. That's just something silly we liked to laugh about - *that* was a game. This isn't, not if what you say is true, not if you intend to do something stupid. And until this stud appeared, you were content enough anyway, even if you *were* unsure about Izzy. If you loved him once, you can again. If you fell out of love, you can fall back in again. Feelings are just fickle, they're no judge

203

of what's really going on and they're not worth trusting. Marriage *is* lonely sometimes, and boring and tedious. That's why we make promises at the beginning.

"Are you really willing to just chuck a perfectly okay marriage out the window? For what? A few laughs and better sex once in a while? It's not just about you any more."

She paused, not sure if Jane was listening or just planning a defence. This was important, she wanted to get it right.

"Maybe Peter wont find out," Jane said, "I'm hardly going to announce it!"

"Jane, they *always* find out," sighed Suzie. "Listen, think hard Jane. Think about the consequences and don't be stupid, please. You are better than that.

"And say that you *did* manage to keep it quiet, is that what you really want? Skulking about, never being honest? Always wondering if you've been seen, desperately trying to remember lies? And you would end up lying to everyone, not just Peter. You'd have to lie to the kids, your mum, friends.

"And what if it continued, what if you fell in love? Are you going to rip apart your family? You can never be rid of Peter you know, you will share those children for the rest of your life. So you can look forward to arguments over birthdays, Christmases, weddings. The children will be caught in the middle, not wanting to take sides, all confused and insecure and wondering if it's their fault. Is that what you want?"

"No," whispered Jane, "but I've been so unhappy lately. I feel like I'm invisible." She swallowed, feeling close to tears. This was horrible. She had thought it would be fun, they'd laugh and plot together. Instead she was being painted as some loose woman, someone nasty. And she wasn't nasty, she was a good person. But she was so lonely, and she needed something, someone, more. Suzie didn't understand, she wasn't listening to what Jane was saying. She hadn't looked for this, but it had happened, and it made her happy. She had a right to feel happy, she was sure she did. She fiddled with her cup, unable to meet her friend's eyes.

"Oh Jane! We all feel like that sometimes. But don't throw away what you've got. You and Peter have shared so much, survived the whole baby thing, built your lives together.

"Maybe Peter isn't happy either," she suggested, "perhaps you need to talk, sort out what you both want. Have you tried telling him how you feel?"

"Yes," mumbled Jane, staring at the table, "but he doesn't hear what I'm saying."

Suzie could see that Jane was near to tears. She reached over and squeezed her hand.

"Poor old you, you are having a rough time. Marriage isn't like they tell you when you're young, is it? It's about lonely evenings and dirty socks mainly! But it's also about sharing, and having someone you can rely on. It's about trust…

"Think carefully Jane," she said. "Marriage is horrid sometimes, that's why people talk about working at it. Doesn't mean it's not worth it though.

"Anyway," she added, "aren't you religious? Can't you pray about it or something?"

"Sure," said Jane, feeling irritated now. She wished she'd never said anything, not tried to involve her friend. Perhaps she wasn't such a good friend after all. Maybe things were only fun if Suzie thought of them. Jane hadn't noticed that before.

"Okay, enough," conceded Suzie. "Bit of a lecture that, wasn't it. I'll stop. I'm only saying it because I care."

They talked for a while about safer topics, the fair, holidays and a new television drama. However, the atmosphere was false and their conversation tense, so they did not order fresh coffee and soon Jane glanced at her phone and announced it was time that she left.

"That went well," thought Suzie with an ironic smile as she watched her friend leave. Then her eyes stung with unexpected tears and she began to frantically sort the coffee cups, determined to control her emotions. Jane was her friend, she didn't want to hurt her. But she couldn't joke about this, couldn't just sit back and be party to something destructive.

Suzie knew well the stigma attached to a child of an unfaithful mother. It was not a topic she ever discussed, burying it safely in the past. Her own parents had divorced when she was ten and she and her brother had followed their mother to live with 'Uncle Steven'. She remembered long nights of silent tears in a bed that smelt foreign, longing to return home. At school she had appeared sullen and uncooperative as she struggled to understand why her parents had split so abruptly, a nagging fear deep within that if she had been better, brighter, less trouble, then maybe both parents would have loved her enough to stay together. No one ever criticised her mother to her face but she heard the whispered discussions at family gatherings, saw the snide expressions on the faces of her father's relatives.

Once, just once, did she encounter her father's rage. As a teenager she had overstayed her curfew and crept home late when she had been staying with her father. As she tiptoed to her room the hallway had been suddenly, cruelly illuminated and her father had faced her, grey eyes flashing in anger.

"Sorry I'm late," she began, "Gary's car broke down and…"

She got no further. His hand slapped the side of her face and she fell hard against the wall.

"You're just like your mother!" he spat and marched to his room.

She had stood, frozen like stone for a long time. The grandfather clock ticked loudly in reprimand, marking each cold minute that passed. Then, like a robot, she went to bed. She washed her face. She cleaned her teeth. She brushed her hair. She changed into a pink nylon nightdress. She lay on her bed, in her father's house. She never forgot those words.

All through an awkward breakfast, their stilted conversation pretending all was normal, she remembered. As she sat through lessons - history, biology, art - those words seared into her brain. She felt as if she were branded, like cattle headed for market.

"Just like your mother." "Just like your mother."

Down long years, those words remained. As an adult she could finally understand her mother's desperate loneliness, the pain of living with a husband who didn't restrain his moods, who flared with anger when he was disobeyed. She could also emphasise with her father's feeling of hurt betrayal, the unexpected loss of the woman who he loved. Yet she could never shake off the fear that some gene of unfaithfulness had been passed on to her, was part of her. It made her cling to the man who adored her trustingly, determined to never be *"Just like your mother."*

Now, as Suzie watched Jane leave, she almost wished she too knew how to pray.

"Don't do it," her mind pleaded, "Just don't bloody do it." She sniffed and stood, extracting a shopping list from her bag. Then she headed towards the supermarket.

#

Jane walked quickly to her car. She felt like a small child who had been reprimanded. She fumbled crossly for her keys.

"She's just jealous," she muttered, throwing her bag onto the back seat. "I didn't ask for her opinion anyway. She doesn't understand me, or how my life is. It was a mistake telling her, and I won't make the same mistake again. This is my life, my business, and I can make my own decisions."

She drove home, glaring at the other cars.

Chapter Twenty-One

The following morning, having completed the school run, Jane drove to the cemetery. She wanted to think and there was something intangibly honest about a graveyard. Death was honest. People could pretend their whole life, act a part which convinced even themselves; but no one could be fake in death. There was a stark truth about the ending of a life, a blatant inability to hide. Jane had felt it at the funeral. Sorrow was awful, but it was real. Sometimes life was so muddled and false that even hurtful clarity was welcome. A half forgotten saying filtered through her mind, something about it being : "Better to attend a funeral than a wedding."

She felt that she almost understood what that meant.

So she chose the graveyard to do her thinking. She walked first to Sophia's grave. She knelt and fingered some fading flowers, the crunchy green oasis showing through where they had shrivelled. A card, damp and curling was still fastened, but Jane did not read it. It would be like prying, spying on a private message.

There were fresh flowers too, white and pink, smiling on the sunken mound of dried earth. She supposed Tricia had placed them there, needing to still do something for her child, needing a way to mourn. The thought of it still took her breath away, she could barely imagine the emptiness that must fill you if you lost a child. You would, she thought, cease to be the same person. So much is invested in our children, they represent our future. It would be like losing a limb.

Jane moved to a wooden bench and sat. She perched her heels on the edge of the seat and hugged her knees. She was quite alone. There was a distant whine of traffic and the occasional growl of an overhead aeroplane but she was watched only by a blackbird as he

209

tugged a worm from the soil. She rested her chin on her folded arms and tried to think.

She thought about her life as it was now. The overwhelming physical bond she shared with her children. She thought about how it felt when Christopher held her face in both small hands, when Abigail confided in her, when they clung to her for comfort. She considered long days of scattered toys, dust and laundry. The tedium of school runs, constant meals, endless shopping.

"Why did you let this happen?" she asked God. "You knew I was lonely, you know that Peter mostly ignores me unless he's feeling randy or wants me to help with something.

"How *many* evenings," she thought, "have I sat alone in a house of sleeping children, while he's off living his life? How many hours do I spend, never speaking to another adult? Is this what I want? Is this what I have become? Someone who enables everyone else to have a life? I am eclipsed by them, by their needs and demands. They don't even see me anymore, not Jane, the person. I am a wife, a mother, a daughter. But I want to be me too, Jane, a person. I am not simply an appendage, a useful add-on.

"It's your fault," she raged at God, "You made Matthew fun and kind to me. You knew I was vulnerable, you knew I was empty inside. And you sent someone who cares but who I can't have. You sent someone who sees me, who likes me for who I am, not because I'm useful to him."

She stopped. If she was honest, she didn't actually know how Matthew saw her. Did he see her, like her, want her company? Or was he looking for something a bit different and bedding a wife and mother would make a change. At least, she assumed it would be a change - again, she didn't really know. It was possible he did this with all his customers, moved from lonely wife to lonely wife….

But she didn't think so. She thought herself a good judge of character, and she was sure he was a good person and had genuinely liked her. He was so good with Christopher, she was sure a philanderer wouldn't be kind to a child. No, it was just Suzie making her doubt things. He liked her, and thought she was special.

"I only want some fun," she reasoned, "I only want to feel human again. Isn't pursuit of happiness a basic human right?"

She thought back to her childhood, hours spent playing with dolls. How lovingly she had dressed them, held plastic spoons to their painted lips. She had washed their plastic faces at bedtime and snuggled them under her own covers. She remembered their unwieldy bodies against her at night, their stiff moulded fingers scratching her face when she rolled against them in her sleep.

One doll, Hilda, she had loved above all others. She had strands of nylon hair that could actually be combed and blue staring eyes fringed with ginger lashes that closed when she was laid down. Once, Jane had trimmed her hair with red handled scissors. The hair had fallen in one clump, leaving a bald patch behind the right ear. Jane had cried and Hilda had always worn a bonnet after that.

Another time, Jane had bathed her in the sink, washing away grime with rose scented bubble bath. She had dried her in a big towel and dressed her in a yellow onesie. All that night, Hilda's hollow legs had leaked tepid water into Jane's bed. The following day she had returned from school to find both her bedding and Hilda hanging on the washing line. She had viewed Daphne as a cruel torturer. It took several days for her to forgive her mother.

Hilda herself never recovered. The water rusted the joints in her hips. Two weeks later, her legs fell off.

"Such futile love," thought Jane, "so much wasted emotion."

Or had that care been good practice, preparing her for the unconditional love of real motherhood? It was all she had ever wanted, to be married, to have children.

"If only I had known how lonely it would be," she thought.

Her thoughts moved to Peter. She could see him as a young man, bursting with vibrant energy, full of ideas. He had *seen* Jane in those days, had noticed everything about her, made her feel special, cherished. Strange word, *cherished*. It was only ever used in the wedding vows, which, it seemed to Jane, was the time when mostly it stopped happening. How many wives actually feel *cherished* by their husbands?

"Did I even choose to marry him?" she wondered, "Or did it just happen? Perhaps I just drifted into marriage, as a logical next step, without even thinking whether I really wanted it. Did I ever consider there might be a different option.

"What do I actually want?" she asked, "Do I want to be free? Do I want to risk losing everything or am I willing to risk stagnating, disappearing into a shape labelled *wife and mother*?"

The answer eluded her, but she knew she wanted to make a decision. She did not want to wander through life anymore. Whichever route she took, it would be of her own choosing, she would not allow herself to drift into an affair, nor would she remain married through passive indecision. She would decide. She would attempt to control her own life.

"I'm not Hilda," she smiled, "I don't have to just let things happen to me."

By the time she left, she was stiff from sitting for so long. As she walked through the graves, around the markers for so many forgotten lives, she felt at peace. Her decision was made. Jane was going home.

Chapter Twenty Two

It was Sunday afternoon. Abigail was hiding upstairs with a book and some chocolate she had found, lying forgotten at the back of the fridge.

Jane had cleared away the remains of lunch and was now snuggled on the sofa with a magazine. She flicked the glossy pages, absorbing colours and moods but not bothering to read the articles. It was one of those deliciously lazy afternoons, where no one could be bothered to do much, and nothing was urgent.

Christopher had spread his train set across the carpet and then gone to find his father. They were working together now, moving in easy silence, constructing the track. Painted trains, one missing a wheel, were pushed in a heap under the table as they joined the pieces to form a route. It stretched from the door to the opposite corner, circling a shoe and curving around a chair. It was decidedly unstable where it climbed to go over a rug and Jane doubted it was structurally sound. She was glad there were no passengers.

She watched Peter's back as he bent to repair the track. The sun caught his hair, highlighting the few white strands. She knew every curve of his body, every crease of his face. The feel and smell of him were as familiar as her own reflection.

"This is what I want," she realised, certain now of her decision. "This is secure, safe, familiar. I can be at peace here, with this man. It may not always be exciting but it lets me be who I want to be."

She knew, deep inside, that her decision had been the right one. She might be ignored sometimes, though was probably not as invisible as she felt. Undoubtedly they would argue and she would be hurt because Peter *was* selfish. But maybe everyone was selfish, some were just better at hiding it. Nor did he understand her fully. But he understood enough, and he did try - she knew that now. As she had evaluated their life together, forced herself to be fair, she knew that if she was to keep a tally of wet towels on the floor and late nights on her own, she also had to note the surprise gifts, the phone calls when he was away, the security of a husband who worked hard.

She still remembered their early days together, the thrill of seeing him. That had worn away now, but would it last forever with anyone? Surely in time, even the most exciting of lovers would become familiar. At the end of the day, she would be swapping a man with - another man, and they were not really so very different at the core.

As father and son played together, intent on their task and oblivious to her thoughts, Jane felt that her whole life had led up to this point. She was deciding to stay. It was her choice. She thought about the smell of Peter, the warmth of his body, the way they fitted together so perfectly when they snuggled. She thought about the shared experiences, how their eyes could say so much to each other, the times they laughed together. It was a lot to risk, a lot to lose.

Peter looked up, smiling to see her watching.

"I could kill for a cup of tea," he said.

As Jane filled the kettle, her bag on the table began to vibrate. She scooped out her mobile phone.

One new message from Matthew' the illuminated screen informed her.

She stood very still, not breathing. The timing was eery. But she had decided. She was staying, and she wasn't going to mess with what she already had.

She pressed 'menu'. She scrolled down to 'messages', selected 'clean up messages' and chose 'all'. Obediently, the phone wiped all messages from its memory.

"I don't owe him anything, not even politeness," thought Jane. "He knew I was married, he knew what he was asking me to gamble, and if he'd really cared, he wouldn't have asked."

Slowly, Jane slipped the phone back into her bag. She would miss him, and for a moment, tears stung her eyes. But she knew she was right, knew that whilst this might not be perfect, it was the better choice. She switched on the kettle and pulled down a purple mug. Outside, a bird began to sing.

Chapter Twenty Three

Jane pulled the shoe off the shelf. White satin, with a tiny bow - it would suit the dress. As she turned towards the fitting room, she glimpsed her reflection in one of the mirrors. Her hair was looking very grey, she hadn't had time to colour her roots for ages. Not that it mattered, the hair appointment had been booked weeks ago, tomorrow they would turn it back to the brown of younger days.

The curtain parted, and Abigail stepped forwards. A beautiful, untouchable Abigail. The white lace dress fell to the floor in waves, a fish-tail train sweeping the floor. The bodice fitted her slim frame, a scalloped neckline revealing glimpses of shoulder.

She grinned at Jane and walked forwards. Her stride was not particularly princess-like, more a stomp as she struggled with the excess material. It reminded Jane of the girl she had been, the way her feet used to turn inwards, how her shoes were always scuffed. Unbidden, tears filled her eyes. It felt like yesterday, and now that determined girl was a young woman. But still her daughter, still a little girl in her heart.

"Do you like it?" said Abigail, noticing her mother's rapid blinks and checking they were for the right reason.

"Yes," said Jane. It was all she *could* say for a moment. She took a breath, and held up the shoes. "What about these?"

Abigail wrinkled her nose. "They're a bit high," she said.

Jane smiled. "I remember when all you wanted were high heels," she said. "Do you remember the shopping trip when you were little and you lost your shoes?"

"They were stolen, actually," said Abigail, smiling too. "Can you unzip me?"

Jane followed her back into the fitting room and helped her daughter out of the wedding gown. It was heavy, and very white, she hoped her hands wouldn't leave a greasy mark. A shop assistant fluttered around, telling Abigail she looked lovely, no alterations were necessary, did she want to take it today? They would box it for her.

When she was dressed in jeans again, she followed Jane to the racks of shoes and started to look.

"It's only a couple of weeks away," said Jane, "you really ought to have sorted shoes by now."

"I know," said Abigail, "I thought it would be easy. No one will really see them anyway under the dress, I could wear trainers…."

Suddenly serious, she turned to Jane. "Mum, am I doing the right thing?"

Jane looked at her. "Wearing trainers? No."

She realised her daughter was serious and stopped. "What do you mean? Are you having second thoughts?" She started to think about the cost, how she would tell Peter, what their friends would say.

Abigail shook her head. "Not about Simon, no - I know I love him and want to be with him. But the whole marriage thing. Lots of people just live together, it feels like a lot of fuss…"

Jane sat down on a plush red sofa. Abigail had wanted a wedding for as long as she could remember. She had loved choosing the stationary and the dress and the venue. This was not about the wedding. She waited.

"I mean," said Abigail, sitting beside her, "what if I can't do it? What if I am making promises that I can't keep? The whole 'until death us do part' bit - well, that's a really long time isn't it! We might change. I know you and Dad have always been happy, but in a way, that makes it harder. What if I'm not made the same, what if I'm not the 'til death us do part' sort?"

Jane reached out and took her daughter's hand.

"Yes, she said, "it is a *really* long time. And sometimes you will wonder what the heck you've signed up for. But it's a decision. Really, love is a decision. I don't think there is one 'Mr Right' who you have to look for until you find him, I expect I could've been happy with a whole host of people. But I chose your father. And sometimes it was difficult, sometimes I regretted that decision, but I chose to stay. Feelings change, people change, you have to decide what you want and stick with it. And yes, you will both change. But if you spend enough time together, you will change together. It's about choosing to move through life as a unit, not two separate people. We can't control what will happen, our health, the economy, politics. But we can choose whether we will face what comes on our own, or with someone else. You have chosen to be with Simon." She smiled. "It's not a bad decision, I think."

"Did you ever wonder?" said Abigail. "Did you ever regret marrying Dad?"

Jane thought a thousand thoughts.

Then she squeezed her daughter's hand and smiled. "More than once! But that's what I mean about it being a decision. Feelings are very unreliable, they come and go and come again. Sometimes you have to stick it out, but then the love and happiness come back, and you're glad you stayed."

She turned, looked her daughter full in the face.

"Marriage isn't easy Abigail. But it is worth it. I wouldn't be without your father for all the world."

Abigail nodded. "Come on, we'll be late and he'll moan." She bent and kissed Jane's forehead. "Thanks Mum."

#

Peter watched as they walked towards him. Abigail was talking, racing ahead, full of decision and purpose. Jane walked next to her, listening. He watched Jane's walk, how she still walked well, even as she had aged.

218

"I still love that woman," he thought to himself, "she is the world to me."

He thought about all the times he could have walked away, the years when money was tight, when the kids were too demanding, when life just seemed like one long treadmill. And he knew there were other women who would've taken her place. Women who smiled a bit too often, were slightly too attentive, suggested drinks after work when no one else would be there. There was even one who had sent him photos of herself, like they had some bond outside of the office. He'd had to put a stop to that, ask for her to be transferred. It was all a bit awkward.

But he'd never considered being unfaithful to Jane. She was his life, his home, the place he escaped to. As he watched her now, with her grey roots and chubby belly, her middle-aged body and lined face, he felt so full of love. It was weird really, watching their kids grow up, Abigail about to be married herself, him thinking about retiring. But Jane was there, the person he had wanted to come home to every day for the last thirty years.

"Funny thing, love," he thought. "You can't really explain it, but it really does make for a happier life."

He stood up as the women approached the table.

"I just hope," he thought, "that Abi's as lucky in her marriage."

Also by Anne E. Thompson

Hidden Faces
Counting Stars
JOANNA

Clara Oakes (due 2018)

See anneethompson.com for details

Read on for an extract from *Counting Stars…*

Chapter One

The Door

The guest house had three stories. She knew this, just as she knew they were connected by both the wide main stairs and the narrow hidden steps originally used by the servants. She chose the wide stairs, her hand skimming the smooth oak bannister as she climbed.

She wanted the third floor. The first two floors were the regular rooms, often used by families who booked two or three of them at a time. There were standard doubles, large twin-bed and tiny single rooms. Each one boasted a sink, but the guests had to leave the safety of their room if they needed the bathroom. There was a selection of bathrooms with over bath showers and single cubicle toilets placed conveniently along both floors.

But the third floor was special. The third floor was where the *en suite* rooms lived. Each room had a double bed, matching furnishings, and a small private bathroom, for guests who could afford the *en suite* tax, who could afford a little luxury. They were at the top of the house (if one does not include the attics, which had been renovated for the staff to use) and they enjoyed a view of the sea. A tiny view. A glimpse really, between the tree tops.

However, it was not to one of these rooms she went. It was to the rather unnecessary extra bathroom. It sat between two rooms, tucked back in an alcove. The wood slatted door was painted to match the other doors and would have been easy to miss, angled as it was away from the landing, almost as if trying to hide. A shy door. But she knew it was there and cautiously opened it.

Inside was what one might expect to see in an upstairs convenience. Behind the door as you entered, on the left, was a white china toilet with high water closet and old fashioned chain for flushing. Opposite it, on your right as you entered, was a white sink. It had been tastefully littered with miniature soaps and scrubbed sea shells.

None of this interested her. It was as she remembered. She went straight to the cupboard. It was set in the wall to the left of the toilet, opposite the door, was raised a good four feet from the floor and reached nearly to the ceiling. The door was tongue and groove, painted white to match the chinaware. There was a small lock on the right, and she was relieved to see the key was still in it. They had always kept it there for fear it would be lost, some traditions never change. It seemed unlikely that a guest would bother to open the door, even if they ventured in to use the toilet.

She reached up and turned the key. It was small and stiff but it ground its way round and the door swung open.

Inside there were no tidy piles of linen or spare toilet rolls. There were steps. Great stone steps which led up and away.

Smiling, she closed and locked the door, putting the key safely in her jeans' pocket. She could feel it there, digging into her hip. She would come back later with the family.

It was dark when she returned, and very late. She first woke the mother who seemed to be expecting her. They spoke little as they gathered some warm clothes, pushing them into a small backpack. Then they woke the children together, the mother going first into the room, hushing them, telling them it was an adventure, they needed to be quiet. She worried they would speak in their high child voices, voices that seem to penetrate so clearly and wake someone. But they were older than she had expected, the boy almost as tall as his mother, at that lanky thin stage that so often precedes manhood. They seemed to catch the mood of the adults and, compliant with sleepiness, they allowed themselves to be dressed and guided up the stairs to the third floor.

She could tell the mother was surprised to be taken into the small washroom. She held her children close to her and watched silently as the door was locked, the key to the cupboard was produced. They all peered in, stared at the steps, wondered if their legs were long enough to climb those big slabs of stone. Would the girl manage? The mother spoke a single word:

"Up?"

She nodded, understanding the question, knowing the answer.

And so they climbed. First onto the lowered lid of the toilet, using it as a first giant step, then into the cupboard. She went last, helping the mother, passing her the girl, helping the boy. She squeezed in behind them, twisting to pull the door shut, turning the key, delaying anyone who might follow. Then they went up and round.

The steps, which you might have assumed, as the mother did, would descend, first went up. The steps climbed steeply, turning as they went, following the line of the chimney breast. Then a straight section, long and thin with a slight draught that made the family shiver. The floor was different here, weathered floorboards, and they knew they were crossing a section of the attic, hidden from view behind the thick stone walls. Then at last, down. The steps were built into the ancient walls, unseen, long forgotten by all but a few.

It was very narrow. The boy caught his elbow on the rough stone wall and cried out, angry with the wall, angry with himself. His sister's eyes grew very large as red blood oozed from the cut, and they wondered if she might cry. The mother touched her hair, comforting and warning in one smooth stroke. Then she bent, sucked the wound clean, her eyes telling the boy to be brave, he was a man now. They continued, down, down. The girl almost jumping, the steps were so tall, clinging onto the back of her mother for support. Down, down. Below the second floor, then the first, then the ground. Into the earth.

The steps finished and they faced a tunnel. Long and dark. A passage with no end. Where monsters might live. She snapped on a torch and the monsters retreated, back into the gloom beyond the beam. They walked on.

The floor was earth, hard and dry. Then stones, then rock, carved by men long ago, deep under the ground. The rock was shiny in places, she worried they might slip and they all took a hand, turning slightly to walk in pairs along the narrow tunnel. On and on where once they had walked down. Not stopping, not speaking, though she knew they could now. For they were under the sea and no one would hear but mermaids and crabs. But what would they say? Words would only stir emotions and they needed to be locked away until there was room to set them free. Later, much later.

The girl started to slow, for the walk was a long one. She thought of her bed, of the dreams she had left, and began to whine, to make tiny whimpering sounds. The boy was silent, just looked at her, his eyes unreadable.

Still they went on. The air was stale and chill but they were moving and not cold. It smelled of sea and salt and mermaid hair. Still holding hands, almost dragging now, wondering if they could make it, wondering how long to go, how far to return.

Finally, they arrived. The passage widened, began to slope upwards, four rough steps hewn from the rock and then sand, soft and damp, clinging to their shoes, creeping into their socks. They came up, out of a cave and she saw they had arrived. The sky was black and starless when she turned off the torch. Their faces were very white.

Still silent she turned. First she hugged the mother, pushing hope and strength into her. Then the girl, lightly and with affection. Then she hugged the boy, roughly, willing him to be brave, to take his father's place. Then she left them, turning swiftly away and dipping back into the cave. They were on their own now.

The Island

The mother led the children away from the cave. They were whimpering now, pleading to sit, to rest a while. Even the boy was making a fuss, his discomfort making him revert to childhood. But it was too cold. They needed to find shelter, if only for what remained of the night. The wind tugged at their clothes, pushed against their exposed faces, tangled their hair.

Counting Stars - an exciting novel set in the world around the corner. Available now from Amazon.

Printed in Great Britain
by Amazon